Samuel Beckett was born in Dublin in 1906. During the 1920s he went to live in Paris, and was a close friend of James Joyce, who regarded him as a very promising writer. He published novels, stories and poems, but did not achieve fame until his play, *Waiting for Godot*, was performed in 1953. Since then he has gained recognition as perhaps the greatest living prose writer, a magnificent novelist as well as playwright. His novels include *Murphy* (1938) – also published in Picador – *Watt* (1944), and the trilogy, *Malone Dies*, *Molloy* and *How It Is* (1959). Among his plays are *End Game* (1957) and *Krapp's Last Tape* (1959). He writes with equal ease in French and English, but his most recent books were originally written in French. Beckett won the Prix Formentor in 1961 for his outstanding contribution to world literature, and the Nobel Prize for Literature in 1969.

Previously published by
Samuel Beckett in Picador

Murphy

Samuel Beckett

More Pricks than Kicks

 published by Pan Books

First published in Great Britain 1934 by
Chatto and Windus Ltd
Limited editions published 1966, 1967 by
Calder and Boyars Ltd.
Republished 1970 by
Calder and Boyars Ltd
This Picador edition published 1974 by
Pan Books Ltd, Cavaye Place, London SW10 9PG
2nd printing 1977
© Samuel Beckett 1934
ISBN 0 330 24159 1
Printed in Great Britain by
Richard Clay (The Chaucer Press), Ltd, Bungay, Suffolk

CONTENTS

DANTE AND THE LOBSTER   7

FINGAL   21

DING-DONG   33

A WET NIGHT   45

LOVE AND LETHE   77

WALKING OUT   91

WHAT A MISFORTUNE   103

THE SMERALDINA'S BILLET DOUX   135

YELLOW   143

DRAFF   159

DANTE AND THE LOBSTER

It was morning and Belacqua was stuck in the first of the canti in the moon. He was so bogged that he could move neither backward nor forward. Blissful Beatrice was there, Dante also, and she explained the spots on the moon to him. She showed him in the first place where he was at fault, then she put up her own explanation. She had it from God, therefore he could rely on its being accurate in every particular. All he had to do was to follow her step by step. Part one, the refutation, was plain sailing. She made her point clearly, she said what she had to say without fuss or loss of time. But part two, the demonstration, was so dense that Belacqua could not make head or tail of it. The disproof, the reproof, that was patent. But then came the proof, a rapid shorthand of the real facts, and Belacqua was bogged indeed. Bored also, impatient to get on to Piccarda. Still he pored over the enigma, he would not concede himself conquered, he would understand at least the meanings of the words, the order in which they were spoken and the nature of the satisfaction that they conferred on the misinformed poet, so that when they were ended he was refreshed and could raise his heavy head, intending to return thanks and make formal retraction of his old opinion.

He was still running his brain against this impenetrable passage when he heard midday strike. At once he switched his mind off its task. He scooped his fingers under the book and shovelled it back till it lay wholly on his palms. The Divine Comedy face upward on the lectern of his palms. Thus disposed he raised it under his nose and there he slammed it shut. He held it aloft for a time, squinting at it angrily, pressing the boards inwards with the heels of his hands. Then he laid it aside.

He leaned back in his chair to feel his mind subside and the itch of this mean quodlibet die down. Nothing could be done until his mind got better and was still, which gradually it did. Then he ventured to consider what he had to do next. There was always something that one had to do next. Three large obligations presented themselves. First lunch, then the lobster, then the Italian lesson. That would do to be going on with. After the Italian lesson he had no very clear idea. No doubt some niggling curriculum had been drawn up by someone for the late afternoon and evening, but he did not know what. In any case it did not matter. What did matter was: one, lunch; two, the lobster; three, the Italian lesson. That was more than enough to be going on with.

Lunch, to come off at all, was a very nice affair. If his lunch was to be enjoyable, and it could be very enjoyable indeed, he must be left in absolute tranquillity to prepare it. But if he were disturbed now, if some brisk tattler were to come bouncing in now with a big idea or a petition, he might just as well not eat at all, for the food would turn to bitterness on his palate or, worse again, taste of nothing. He must be left strictly alone, he must have complete quiet and privacy, to prepare the food for his lunch.

The first thing to do was to lock the door. Now nobody could come at him. He deployed an old Herald and smoothed it out on the table. The rather handsome face of McCabe the assassin stared up at him. Then he lit the gas-ring and unhooked the square flat toaster, asbestos grill, from its nail and set it precisely on the flame. He found he had to lower the flame. Toast must not on any account be done too rapidly. For bread to be toasted as it ought, through and through, it must be done on a mild steady flame. Otherwise you only charred the outsides and left the pith as sodden as before. If there was one thing he abominated more than another it was to feel his teeth meet in a bathos of pith and dough. And it was so easy to do the thing properly. So, he thought, having regulated the flow and adjusted the grill, by the time I have the bread cut that will be just right. Now the long barrel-loaf came out of its biscuit-tin and had its end evened off on the face of McCabe. Two inexorable drives with the bread-saw and a pair of neat rounds of raw bread, the main elements of his meal, lay before him, awaiting his pleasure. The stump of the loaf went back into prison, the crumbs, as though there were no such thing as a sparrow in the wide world, were swept in a fever away, and the slices snatched up and carried to the grill. All these preliminaries were very hasty and impersonal.

It was now that real skill began to be required, it was at this point that the average person began to make a hash of the entire proceedings. He laid his cheek against the soft of the bread, it was spongy and warm, alive. But he would very soon take that plush feel off it, by God but he would very quickly take that fat white look off its face. He lowered the gas a suspicion and plaqued one flabby slab plump down on the glowing fabric, but very pat and precise, so that the whole resembled the Japanese flag. Then on top, there not being room for the two to do evenly side by side, and if you did not do them evenly you might just as well save yourself the trouble of doing them at all, the other round was set to warm. When the first candidate was done, which was only when it was black through and through, it changed places with its comrade, so that now it in its turn lay on top, done to a dead end, black and smoking, waiting till as much could be said of the other.

For the tiller of the field the thing was simple, he had it from his mother. The spots were Cain with his truss of thorns, dispossessed, cursed from the earth, fugitive and vagabond. The moon was that countenance fallen and branded, seared with the first stigma of God's pity, that an outcast might not die quickly. It was a mix-up in the mind of the tiller, but that did not matter. It had been good enough for his mother, it was good enough for him.

Belacqua on his knees before the flame, poring over the grill, controlled every phase of the broiling. It took time, but if a thing was worth doing at all it was worth doing well, that was a true saying. Long before the end the room was full of smoke and the reek of burning. He switched off the gas, when all that human care and skill could do had been done, and restored the toaster to its nail. This was an act of dilapidation, for it seared a great weal in the paper. This was hooliganism pure and simple. What the hell did he care? Was it his wall? The same hopeless paper had been there fifty years. It was livid with age. It could not be disimproved.

Next a thick paste of Savora, salt and Cayenne on each round, well worked in while the pores were still open with the heat. No butter, God forbid, just a good forment of mustard and salt and pepper on each round. Butter was a blunder, it made the toast soggy. Buttered toast was all right for Senior Fellows and Salvationists, for such as had nothing but false teeth in their heads. It was no good at all to a fairly strong young rose like Belacqua. This meal that he was at such pains to make ready, he would devour it with a sense of rapture and victory, it would be like smiting the sledded Polacks on the ice. He would snap at it with closed eyes, he would gnash it into a pulp, he would vanquish it utterly with his fangs. Then the anguish of pungency, the pang of the spices, as each mouthful died, scorching his palate, bringing tears.

But he was not yet all set, there was yet much to be done. He had burnt his offering, he had not fully dressed it. Yes, he had put the horse behind the tumbrel.

He clapped the toasted rounds together, he brought them smartly together like cymbals, they clave the one to the other on the viscid salve of Savora. Then he wrapped them up for the time being in any old sheet of paper. Then he made himself ready for the road.

Now the great thing was to avoid being accosted. To be stopped at this stage and have conversational nuisance committed all over him would be a disaster. His whole being was straining forward towards the joy in store. If he were accosted now he might just as well fling his lunch into the gutter and walk straight back home. Sometimes his hunger, more of mind, I need scarcely say, than of body, for this meal amounted to such a frenzy that he would not have hesitated to strike any man rash enough to buttonhole and baulk him, he would have shouldered him out of his path without ceremony. Woe betide the meddler who crossed him when his mind was really set on this meal.

He threaded his way rapidly, his head bowed, through a familiar labyrinth of lanes and suddenly dived into a little family grocery. In the shop they were not surprised. Most days, about this hour, he shot in off the street in this way.

The slab of cheese was prepared. Separated since morning from the piece, it was only waiting for Belacqua to call and take it. Gorgonzola cheese. He knew a man who came from Gorgonzola, his name was Angelo. He had been born in Nice but all his youth had been spent in Gorgonzola. He knew where to look for it. Every day it was there, in the same corner, waiting to be called for. They were very decent obliging people.

He looked sceptically at the cut of cheese. He turned it over on its back to see was the other side any better. The other side was worse. They had laid it better side up, they had practised that little deception. Who shall blame them? He rubbed it. It was sweating. That was something. He stooped and smelt it. A faint fragrance of corruption. What good was that? He didn't want fragrance, he wasn't a bloody gourmet, he wanted a good stench. What he wanted was a good green stenching rotten lump of Gorgonzola cheese, alive, and by God he would have it.

He looked fiercely at the grocer.

'What's that?' he demanded.

The grocer writhed.

'Well?' demanded Belacqua, he was without fear when roused, 'is that the best you can do?'

'In the length and breadth of Dublin' said the grocer 'you won't find a rottener bit this minute.'

Belacqua was furious. The impudent dogsbody, for two pins he would assault him.

'It won't do' he cried, 'do you hear me, it won't do at all. I won't have it.' He ground his teeth.

The grocer, instead of simply washing his hands like Pilate, flung out his arms in a wild crucified gesture of supplication. Sullenly Belacqua undid his packet and slipped the cadaverous tablet of cheese between the hard cold black boards of the toast. He stumped to the door where he whirled round however.

'You heard me?' he cried.

'Sir' said the grocer. This was not a question, nor yet an expression of acquiescence. The tone in which it was let fall made it quite impossible to know what was in the man's mind. It was a most ingenious riposte.

'I tell you' said Belacqua with great heat 'this won't do at all. If you can't do better than this' he raised the hand that held the packet 'I shall be obliged to go for my cheese elsewhere. Do you mark me?'

'Sir' said the grocer.

He came to the threshold of his store and watched the indignant customer hobble away. Belacqua had a spavined gait, his feet were in ruins, he suffered with them almost continuously. Even in the night they took over from the corns and hammer-toes, and carried on. So that he would press the fringes of his feet desperately against the end-rail of the bed or better again, reach down with his hand and drag them up and back towards the instep. Skill and patience could disperse the pain, but there it was, complicating his night's rest.

The grocer, without closing his eyes or taking them off the receding figure, blew his nose in the skirt of his apron. Being a warm-hearted human man he felt sympathy and pity for this queer customer who always looked ill and dejected. But at the same time he was a small tradesman, don't forget that, with a small tradesman's sense of personal dignity and what was what. Thruppence, he cast it up, thruppence worth of cheese per day, one and a tanner per week. No, he would fawn on no man for that, no, not on the best in the land. He had his pride.

Stumbling along by devious ways towards the lowly public where he was expected, in the sense that the entry of his grotesque person would provoke no comment or laughter, Belacqua gradually got the upper hand of his choler. Now that lunch was as good as a fait accompli, because the incontinent bosthoons of his own class, itching to pass on a big idea or inflict an appointment, were seldom at large in this shabby quarter of the city, he was free to consider items two and three, the lobster and the lesson, in closer detail.

At a quarter to three he was due at the School. Say five to three. The public closed, the fishmonger reopened, at half-past two. Assuming then that his lousy old bitch of an aunt had given her order in good time that morning, with strict injunctions that it should be ready and waiting so that her blackguard boy should on no account be delayed when he called for it first thing in the afternoon, it would be time enough if he left the public as it closed, he could remain on till the last moment. Benissimo. He had half-a-crown. That was two pints of draught anyway and perhaps a bottle to wind up with. Their bottled stout was particularly excellent and well up. And he would still be left with enough coppers to buy a Herald and take a tram if he felt tired or was pinched for time. Always assuming, of course, that the lobster was all ready to be handed over. God damn these tradesmen, he thought, you can never rely on them. He had not done an exercise but that did not matter. His Professoressa was so charming and remarkable. Signorina Adriana Ottolenghi! He did not believe it possible for a woman to be more intelligent or better informed than the little Ottolenghi. So he had set her on a pedestal in his mind, apart from other women. She had said last day that they would read Il Cinque Maggio together. But she would not mind if he told her, as he proposed to, in Italian, he would frame a shining phrase on his way from the public, that he would prefer to postpone the Cinque Maggio to another occasion. Manzoni was an old woman, Napoleon was another. Napoleone di mezza calzetta, fa l'amore a Giacominetta. Why did he think of Manzoni as an old woman? Why did he do him that injustice? Pellico was another. They were all old maids, suffragettes. He must ask his Signorina where he could have received that impression, that the nineteenth century in Italy was full of old hens trying to cluck like Pindar. Carducci was another. Also about the spots on the moon. If she could not tell him there and then she would make it up, only too gladly, against the next time. Everything was all set now and in order. Bating, of course, the lobster, which had to remain an incalculable factor. He must just hope for the best. And expect the worst, he thought gaily, diving into the public, as usual.

Belacqua drew near to the school, quite happy, for all had gone swimmingly. The lunch had been a noticeable success, it would abide as a standard in his mind. Indeed he could not imagine its ever being superseded. And such a pale soapy piece of cheese to prove so strong! He must only conclude that he had been abusing himself all these years in relating the strength of cheese directly to its greenness. We live and learn, that was a true saying. Also his teeth and jaws had been in heaven, splinters of vanquished toast spraying forth at each gnash. It was like eating glass. His mouth burned and ached with the exploit. Then the food had been further spiced by the intelligence, transmitted in a low tragic voice across the counter by Oliver the improver, that the Malahide murderer's petition for mercy, signed by half the land, having been rejected, the man must swing at dawn in Mountjoy and nothing could save him. Ellis the hangman was even now on his way. Belacqua, tearing at the sandwich and swilling the precious stout, pondered on McCabe in his cell.

The lobster was ready after all, the man handed it over instanter, and with such a pleasant smile. Really a little bit of courtesy and goodwill went a long way in this world. A smile and a cheerful word from a common working-man and the face of the world was brightened. And it was so easy, a mere question of muscular control.

'Lepping' he said cheerfully, handing it over.

'Lepping?' said Belacqua. What on earth was that?

'Lepping fresh, sir' said the man, 'fresh in this morning.'

Now Belacqua, on the analogy of mackerel and other fish that he had heard described as lepping fresh when they had been taken but an hour or two previously, supposed the man to mean that the lobster had very recently been killed.

Signorina Adriana Ottolenghi was waiting in the little front room off the hall, which Belacqua was naturally inclined to think of rather as the vestibule. That was her room, the Italian room. On the same side, but at the back, was the French room. God knows where the German room was. Who cared about the German room anyway?

He hung up his coat and hat, laid the long knobby brown-paper parcel on the hall-table, and went prestly in to the Ottolenghi.

After about half-an-hour of this and that obiter, she complimented him on his grasp of the language.

'You make rapid progress' she said in her ruined voice.

There subsisted as much of the Ottolenghi as might be expected to the person of a lady of a certain age who had found being young and beautiful and pure more of a bore than anything else.

Belacqua, dissembling his great pleasure, laid open the moon enigma.

'Yes' she said 'I know the passage. It is a famous teaser. Off-hand I cannot tell you, but I will look it up when I get home.'

The sweet creature! She would look it up in her big Dante when she got home. What a woman!

'It occurred to me' she said 'apropos of I don't know what, that you might do worse than make up Dante's rare movements of compassion in Hell. That used to be' her past tenses were always sorrowful 'a favourite question.'

He assumed an expression of profundity.

'In that connexion' he said 'I recall one superb pun anyway: "qui vive la pietà quando è ben morta ..." '

She said nothing.

'Is it not a great phrase?' he gushed.

She said nothing.

'Now' he said like a fool 'I wonder how you could translate that?'

Still she said nothing. Then:

'Do you think' she murmured 'it is absolutely necessary to translate it?'

Sounds as of conflict were borne in from the hall. Then silence. A knuckle tambourined on the door, it flew open and lo it was Mlle Glain, the French instructress, clutching her cat, her eyes out on stalks, in a state of the greatest agitation.

'Oh' she gasped 'forgive me. I intrude, but what was in the bag?'

'The bag?' said the Ottolenghi.

Mlle Glain took a French step forward.

'The parcel' she buried her face in the cat 'the parcel in the hall.'

Belacqua spoke up composedly.

'Mine' he said, 'a fish.'

He did not know the French for lobster. Fish would do very well. Fish had been good enough for Jesus Christ, Son of God, Saviour. It was good enough for Mlle Glain.

'Oh' said Mlle Glain, inexpressibly relieved, 'I caught him in the nick of time.' She administered a tap to the cat. 'He would have tore it to flitters.'

Belacqua began to feel a little anxious.

'Did he actually get at it?' he said.

'No no' said Mlle Glain 'I caught him just in time. But I did not know' with a bluestocking snigger 'what it might be, so I thought I had better come and ask.'

Base prying bitch.

The Ottolenghi was faintly amused.

'Puisqu'il n'y a pas de mal ...' she said with great fatigue and elegance.

'Heureusement' it was clear at once that Mlle Glain was devout 'heureusement'.

Chastening the cat with little skelps she took herself off. The grey hairs of her maidenhead screamed at Belacqua. A devout, virginal bluestocking, honing after a penny's worth of scandal.

'Where were we?' said Belacqua.

But Neapolitan patience has its limits.

'Where are we ever?' cried the Ottolenghi, 'where we were, as we were.'

Belacqua drew near to the house of his aunt. Let us call it Winter, that dusk may fall now and a moon rise. At the corner of the street a horse was down and a man sat on its head. I know, thought Belacqua, that that is considered the right thing to do. But why? A lamplighter flew by on his bike, tilting with his pole at the standards, jousting a little yellow light into the evening. A poorly-dressed couple stood in the bay of a pretentious gateway, she sagging against the railings, her head lowered, he standing facing her. He stood up close to her, his hands dangled by his sides. Where we were, thought Belacqua, as we were. He walked on, gripping his parcel. Why not piety and pity both, even down below? Why not mercy and Godliness together? A little mercy in the stress of sacrifice, a little mercy to rejoice against judgment. He thought of Jonah and the gourd and the pity of a jealous God on Nineveh. And poor McCabe, he would get it in the neck at dawn. What was he doing now, how was he feeling? He would relish one more meal, one more night.

His aunt was in the garden, tending whatever flowers die at that time of year. She embraced him and together they went down into the bowels of the earth, into the kitchen in the basement. She took the parcel and undid it and abruptly the lobster was on the table, on the oilcloth, discovered.

'They assured me it was fresh' said Belacqua.

Suddenly he saw the creature move, this neuter creature. Definitely it changed its position. His hand flew to his mouth.

'Christ!' he said 'it's alive.'

His aunt looked at the lobster. It moved again. It made a faint nervous act of life on the oilcloth. They stood above it, looking down on it, exposed cruciform on the oilcloth. It shuddered again. Belacqua felt he would be sick.

'My God' he whined 'it's alive, what'll we do?'

The aunt simply had to laugh. She bustled off to the pantry to fetch her smart apron, leaving him goggling down at the lobster, and came back with it on and her sleeves rolled up, all business.

'Well' she said 'it is to be hoped so, indeed.'

'All this time' muttered Belacqua. Then, suddenly aware of her hideous equipment: 'What are you going to do?' he cried.

'Boil the beast' she said, 'what else?'

'But it's not dead' protested Belacqua 'you can't boil it like that.'

She looked at him in astonishment. Had he taken leave of his senses.

'Have sense' she said sharply, 'lobsters are always boiled alive. They must be.' She caught up the lobster and laid it on its back. It trembled. 'They feel nothing' she said.

In the depths of the sea it had crept into the cruel pot. For hours, in the midst of its enemies, it had breathed secretly. It had survived the Frenchwoman's cat and his witless clutch. Now it was going alive into scalding water. It had to. Take into the air my quiet breath.

Belacqua looked at the old parchment of her face, grey in the dim kitchen.

'You make a fuss' she said angrily 'and upset me and then lash into it for your dinner.'

She lifted the lobster clear of the table. It had about thirty seconds to live.

Well, thought Belacqua, it's a quick death, God help us all.

It is not.

FINGAL

THE LAST GIRL he went with, before a memorable fit of laughing incapacitated him from gallantry for some time, was pretty, hot and witty, in that order. So one fine Spring morning he brought her out into the country, to the Hill of Feltrim in the country. They turned east off the road from Dublin to Malahide short of the Castle woods and soon it came into view, not much more than a burrow, the ruin of a mill on the top, choked lairs of furze and brambles passim on its gentle slopes. It was a landmark for miles around on account of the high ruin. The Hill of the Wolves.

They had not been very long on the top before he began to feel a very sad animal indeed. But she was to all appearance in high spirits, enjoying the warm sun and the prospect.

'The Dublin mountains' she said 'don't they look lovely, so dreamy.'

Now Belacqua was looking intently in the opposite direction, across the estuary.

'It's the east wind' he said.

She began to admire this and that, the ridge of Lambay Island, rising out of the brown woods of the Castle, Ireland's Eye like a shark, and the ridiculous little hills far away to the north, what were they?

'The Naul' said Belacqua. 'Is it possible you didn't know the Naul?' This in the shocked tone of the travelled spinster: 'You don't say you were in Milan (to rime with villain) and never saw the Cena?' 'Can it be possible that you passed through Chambéry and never called on Mme de Warens?'

'Fingal dull!' he said. 'Winnie you astonish me.'

They considered Fingal for a time together in silence. Its coast eaten away with creeks and marshes, tesserae of small fields, patches of wood springing up like a weed, the line of hills too low to close the view.

'When it's a magic land' he sighed 'like Saône-et-Loire.'

'That means nothing to me' said Winnie.

'Oh yes' he said, 'bons vins et Lamartine, a champaign land for the sad and serious, not a bloody little toy Kindergarten like Wicklow.'

You make great play with your short stay abroad, thought Winnie.

'You and your sad and serious' she said. 'Will you never come off it?'

'Well' he said 'I'll give you Alphonse.'

She replied that he could keep him. Things were beginning to blow up nasty.

'What's that on your face?' she said sharply.

'Impetigo' said Belacqua. He had felt it coming with a terrible itch in the night and in the morning it was there. Soon it would be a scab.

'And you kiss me' she exclaimed 'with that on your face.'

'I forgot' he said. 'I get so excited you know.'

She spittled on her handkerchief and wiped her mouth. Belacqua lay humbly beside her, expecting her to get up and leave him. But instead she said:

'What is it anyway? What does it come from?'

'Dirt' said Belacqua, 'you see it on slum children.'

A long awkward silence followed these words.

'Don't pick it darling' she said unexpectedly at last, 'you'll only make it worse.'

This came to Belacqua like a drink of water to drink in a dungeon. Her goodwill must have meant something to him. He returned to Fingal to cover his confusion.

'I often come to this hill' he said 'to have a view of Fingal, and each time I see it more as a back-land, a land of sanctuary, a land that you don't have to dress up to, that you can walk on in a lounge suit, smoking a cigar.' What a geyser, she thought. 'And where much has been suffered in secret, especially by women.'

'This is all a dream' she said. 'I see nothing but three acres and cows. You can't have Cincinnatus without a furrow.'

Now it was she who was sulky and he who was happy.

'Oh Winnie' he made a vague clutch at her sincerities, for she was all anyway on the grass, 'you look very Roman this minute.'

'He loves me' she said, in earnest jest.

'Only pout' he begged, 'be Roman, and we'll go on across the estuary.'

'And then . . . ?'

And then! Winnie take thought!

'I see' he said 'you take thought. Shall we execute a contract?'

'No need' she said.

He was as wax in her hands, she twisted him this way and that. But now their moods were in accordance, things were somehow very pleasant all of a sudden. She gazed long at the area of contention and he willed her not to speak, to remain there with her grave face, a quiet puella in a blurred world. But she spoke (who shall silence them, at last?), saying that she saw nothing but the grey fields of serfs and the ramparts of ex-favourites. Saw! They were all the same when it came to the pinch – clods. If she closed her eyes she might see something. He would drop the subject, he would not try to communicate Fingal, he would lock it up in his mind. So much the better.

'Look' he pointed.

She looked, blinking for the focus.

'The big red building' he said 'across the water, with the towers.'

At last she thought she saw what he meant.

'Far away' she said 'with the round tower?'

'Do you know what that is' he said 'because my heart's right there.'

Well, she thought, you lay your cards on the table.

'No' she said, 'it looks like a bread factory to me.'

'The Portrane Lunatic Asylum' he said.

'Oh' she said 'I know a doctor there.'

Thus, she having a friend, he his heart, in Portrane, they agreed to make for there.

They followed the estuary all the way round, admiring the theories of swans and the coots, over the dunes and past the Martello tower, so that they came on Portrane from the south and the sea instead of like a vehicle by the railway bridge and the horrible red chapel of Donabate. The place was as full of towers as Dun Laoghaire of steeples: two Martello, the red ones of the asylum, a watertower and the round. Trespassing unawares, for the notice-board was further on towards the coastguard station, they climbed the rising ground to this latter. They followed the grass margin of a ploughed field till they came to where a bicycle was lying, half hidden in the rank grass. Belacqua, who could on no account resist a bicycle, thought what an extraordinary place to come across one. The owner was out in the field, scarifying the dry furrows with a fork.

'Is this right for the tower?' cried Belacqua.

The man turned his head.

'Can we get up to the tower?' cried Belacqua.

The man straightened up and pointed.

'Fire ahead' he said.

'Over the wall?' cried Belacqua. There was no need for him to shout. A conversational tone would have been heard across the quiet field. But he was so anxious to make himself clear, he so dreaded the thought of having to repeat himself, that he not merely raised his voice, but put on a flat accent that astonished Winnie.

'Don't be an eejit' she said, 'if it's straight on it's over the wall.'

But the man seemed pleased that the wall had been mentioned, or perhaps he was just glad of an opportunity to leave his work, for he dropped his fork and came lumbering over to where they were standing. There was nothing at all noteworthy about his appearance. He said that their way lay straight ahead, yes, over the wall, and then the tower was on top of the field, or else they could go back till they came to the road and go along it till they came to the Banks and follow up the Banks. The Banks? Was this fellow one of the more harmless lunatics? Belacqua asked was the tower an old one, as though it required a Dr Petrie to see that it was not. The man said it had been built for relief in the year of the Famine, so he had heard, by a Mrs Somebody whose name he misremembered in honour of her husband.

'Well Winnie' said Belacqua, 'over the wall or follow up the Banks?'

'There's a rare view of Lambay from the top' said the man.

Winnie was in favour of the wall, she thought that it would be more direct now that they had come so far. The man began to work this out. Belacqua had no one but himself to blame if they never got away from this machine.

'But I would like to see the Banks' he said.

'If we went on now' said Winnie 'now that we have come so far, and followed the Banks down, how would that be?'

They agreed, Belacqua and the man, that it needed a woman to think these things out. Suddenly there was a tie between them.

The tower began well; that was the funeral meats. But from the door up it was all relief and no honour; that was the marriage tables.

They had not been long on the top before Belacqua was a sad animal again. They sat on the grass with their faces to the sea and the asylum was all below and behind them.

'Right enough' said Winnie 'I never saw Lambay look so close.'

Belacqua could see the man scraping away at his furrow and felt a sudden longing to be down there in the clay, lending a hand. He checked the explanation of this that was beginning and looked at the soft chord of yellow on the slope, gorse and ragwort juxtaposed.

'The lovely ruins' said Winnie 'there on the left, covered with ivy.' Of a church and, two small fields further on, a square bawnless tower.

'That' said Belacqua 'is where I have sursum corda.'

'Then hadn't we better be getting on' said Winnie, quick as lightning.

'This absurd tower' he said, now that he had been told, 'is before the asylum, and they are before the tower.' He didn't say! 'The crenels on the wall I find as moving...'

Now the loonies poured out into the sun, the better behaved left to their own devices, the others in herds in charge of warders. The whistle blew and the herd stopped; again, and it proceeded.

'As moving' he said 'and moving in the same way, as the colour of the brick in the old mill at Feltrim.'

Who shall silence them, at last?

'It's pinked' continued Belacqua, 'and as a little fat overfed boy I sat on the floor with a hammer and a pinking-iron, scalloping the edge of a red cloth.'

'What ails you?' asked Winnie.

He had allowed himself to get run down, but he scoffed at the idea of a sequitur from his body to his mind.

'I must be getting old and tired' he said 'when I find the nature outside me compensating for the nature inside me, like Jean-Jacques sprawling in a bed of saxifrages.'

'Appearing to compensate' she said. She was not sure what she meant by this, but it sounded well.

'And then' he said 'I want very much to be back in the caul, on my back in the dark for ever.'

'A short ever' she said 'and working day and night.'

The beastly punctilio of women.

'Damn it' he said 'you know what I mean. No shaving or haggling or cold or hugger-mugger, no' – he cast about for a term of ample connotation – 'no night-sweats.'

Below in the playground on their right some of the milder patients were kicking a football. Others were lounging about, alone and in knots, taking their ease in the sun. The head of one appeared over the wall, the hands on the wall, the cheek on the hands. Another, he must have been a very tame one, came half-way up the slope, disappeared into a hollow, emerged after a moment and went back the way he had come. Another, his back turned to them, stood fumbling at the wall that divided the grounds of the asylum from the field where they were. One of the gangs was walking round and round the playground. Below on the other hand a long line of workmen's dwellings, in the gardens children playing and crying. Abstract the asylum and there was little left of Portrane but ruins.

Winnie remarked that the lunatics seemed very sane and well-behaved to her. Belacqua agreed, but he thought that the head over the wall told a tale. Landscapes were of interest to Belacqua only in so far as they furnished him with a pretext for a long face.

Suddenly the owner of the bicycle was running towards them up the hill, grasping the fork. He came barging over the wall, through the chord of yellow and pounding along the crest of the slope. Belacqua rose feebly to his feet. This maniac, with the strength of ten men at least, who should withstand him? He would beat him into a puddle with his fork and violate Winnie. But he bore away as he drew near, for a moment they could hear his panting, and plunged on over the shoulder of the rise. Gathering speed on the down grade, he darted through the gate in the wall and disappeared round a corner of the building. Belacqua looked at Winnie, whom he found staring down at where the man had as it were gone to ground, and then away at the distant point where he had watched him scraping his furrows and been envious. The nickel of the bike sparkled in the sun.

The next thing was Winnie waving and halloing. Belacqua turned and saw a man walking smartly towards them up the slope from the asylum.

'Dr Sholto' said Winnie.

Dr Sholto was some years younger than Belacqua, a pale dark man with a brow. He was delighted – how would he say? – at so unexpected a pleasure, honoured he was sure to make the acquaintance of any friend of Miss Coates. Now they would do him the favour to adjourn . . . ? This meant drink. But Belacqua, having other fish to fry, sighed and improvised a long courteous statement to the effect that there was a point in connexion with the church which he was most anxious to check at first hand, so that if he might accept on behalf of Miss Coates, who was surely tired after her long walk from Malahide . . .

'Malahide!' ejaculated Dr Sholto.

. . . and be himself excused, they could all three meet at the main entrance of the asylum in, say, an hour. How would that be? Dr Sholto demurred politely. Winnie thought hard and said nothing.

'I'll go down by the Banks' said Belacqua agreeably 'and follow the road round. Au revoir.'

They stood for a moment watching him depart. When he ventured to look back they were gone. He changed his course and came to where the bicycle lay in the grass. It was a fine light machine, with red tyres and wooden rims. He ran down the margin to the road and it bounded alongside under his hand. He mounted and they flew down the hill and round the corner till they came at length to the stile that led into the field where the church was. The machine was a treat to ride, on his right hand the sea was foaming among the rocks, the sands ahead were another yellow again, beyond them in the distance the cottages of Rush were bright white, Belacqua's sadness fell from him like a shift. He carried the bicycle into the field and laid it down on the grass. He hastened on foot, without so much as a glance at the church, across the fields, over a wall and a ditch, and stood before the poor wooden door of the tower. The locked appearance of this did not deter him. He gave it a kick, it swung open and he went in.

Meantime Dr Sholto, in his pleasantly appointed sanctum, improved the occasion with Miss Winifred Coates. Thus they were all met together in Portrane, Winnie, Belacqua, his heart and Dr Sholto, and paired off to the satisfaction of all parties. Surely it is in such little adjustments that the benevolence of the First Cause appears beyond dispute. Winnie kept her eye on the time and arrived punctually with her friend at the main entrance. There was no sign of her other friend.

'Late' said Winnie 'as usual.'

In respect of Belacqua Sholto felt nothing but rancour.

'Pah' he said, 'he'll be sandpapering a tomb.'

A stout block of an old man in shirt sleeves and slippers was leaning against the wall of the field. Winnie still sees, as vividly as when then they met her anxious gaze for the first time, his great purple face and white moustaches. Had he seen a stranger about, a pale fat man in a black leather coat.

'No miss' he said.

'Well' said Winnie, settling herself on the wall, to Sholto, 'I suppose he's about somewhere.'

A land of sanctuary, he had said, where much had been suffered secretly. Yes, the last ditch.

'You stay here' said Sholto, madness and evil in his heart, 'and I'll take a look in the church.'

The old man had been showing signs of excitement.

'Is it an escape?' he enquired hopefully.

'No no' said Winnie, 'just a friend.'

But he was off, he was unsluiced.

'I was born on Lambay' he said, by way of opening to an endless story of a recapture in which he had distinguished himself, 'and I've worked here man and boy.'

'In that case' said Winnie 'maybe you can tell me what the ruins are.'

'That's the church' he said, pointing to the near one, it had just absorbed Sholto, 'and that ' pointing to the far one, ' 's the tower.'

'Yes' said Winnie 'but what tower, what was it?'

'The best I know' he said 'is some Lady Something had it.'

This was news indeed.

'Then before that again' it all came back to him with a rush 'you might have heard tell of Dane Swift, he kep a' – he checked the word and then let it come regardless – 'he kep a motte in it.'

'A moth?' exclaimed Winnie.

'A motte' he said 'of the name of Stella.'

Winnie stared out across the grey field. No sign of Sholto, nor of Belacqua, only this puce mass up against her and a tale of a motte and a star. What was a motte?

'You mean' she said 'that he lived there with a woman?'

'He kep her there' said the old man, he had read it in an old Telegraph and he would adhere to it, 'and came down from Dublin.'

Little fat Presto, he would set out early in the morning, fresh and fasting, and walk like camomile.

Sholto appeared on the stile in the crenellated wall, waving blankly. Winnie began to feel that she had made a mess of it.

'God knows' she said to Sholto when he came up 'where he is.'

'You can't hang around here all night' he said. 'Let me drive you home, I have to go up to Dublin anyhow.'

'I can't leave him' wailed Winnie.

'But he's not here, damn it' said Sholto, 'if he was he'd be here.'

The old man, who knew his Sholto, stepped into the breach with a tender of his services: he would keep his eyes open.

'Now' said Sholto, 'he can't expect you to wait here for ever.'

A young man on a bicycle came slowly round the corner from the Donabate direction, saluted the group and was turning into the drive of the asylum.

'Tom' cried Sholto.

Tom dismounted. Sholto gave a brief satirical description of Belacqua's person.

'You didn't see that on the road' he said 'did you?'

'I passed the felly of it on a bike' said Tom, pleased to be of use, 'at Ross's gate, going like flames.'

'On a BIKE!' cried Winnie. 'But he hadn't a bike.'

'Tom' said Sholto 'get out the car, look sharp now and run her down here.'

'But it can't have been him' Winnie was furious for several reasons, 'I tell you he had no bike.'

'Whoever it is' said Sholto, master of the situation, 'we'll pass him before he gets to the main road.'

But Sholto had underestimated the speed of his man, who was safe in Taylor's public-house in Swords, drinking and laughing in a way that Mr Taylor did not like, before they were well on their way.

DING-DONG

My SOMETIME FRIEND Belacqua enlivened the last phase of his solipsism, before he toed the line and began to relish the world, with the belief that the best thing he had to do was to move constantly from place to place. He did not know how this conclusion had been gained, but that it was not thanks to his preferring one place to another he felt sure. He was pleased to think that he could give what he called the Furies the slip by merely setting himself in motion. But as for sites, one was as good as another, because they all disappeared as soon as he came to rest in them. The mere act of rising and going, irrespective of whence and whither, did him good. That was so. He was sorry that he did not enjoy the means to indulge this humour as he would have wished, on a large scale, on land and sea. Hither and thither on land and sea! He could not afford that, for he was poor. But in a small way he did what he could. From the ingle to the window, from the nursery to the bedroom, even from one quarter of the town to another, and back, these little acts of motion he was in a fair way of making, and they certainly did do him some good as a rule. It was the old story of the salad days, torment in the terms and in the intervals a measure of ease.

Being by nature however sinfully indolent, bogged in indolence, asking nothing better than to stay put at the good pleasure of what he called the Furies, he was at times tempted to wonder whether the remedy were not rather more disagreeable than the complaint. But he could only suppose that it was not, seeing that he continued to have recourse to it, in a small way it is true, but nevertheless for years he continued to have recourse to it, and to return thanks for the little good it did him.

The simplest form of this exercise was boomerang, out and back; nay, it was the only one that he could afford for many years. Thus it is clear that his contrivance did not proceed from any discrimination between different points in space, since he returned directly, if we except an occasional pause for refreshment, to his point of departure, and truly no less recruited in spirit than if the interval had been whiled away abroad in the most highly-reputed cities.

I know all this because he told me. We were Pylades and Orestes for a period, flattened down to something very genteel; but the relation abode and was highly confidential while it lasted. I have witnessed every stage of the exercise. I have been there when he set out, springing up and hastening away without as much as by your leave, impelled by some force that he did not care to gainsay. I have had glimpses of him enjoying his little trajectory. I have been there again when he returned, transfigured and transformed. It was very nearly the reverse of the author of the Imitation's 'glad going out and sad coming in'.

He was at pains to make it clear to me, and to all those to whom he exposed his manoeuvre, that it was in no way cognate with the popular act of brute labour, digging and such like, exploited to disperse the dumps, an antidote depending for its efficaciousness on mere physical exhaustion, and for which he expressed the greatest contempt. He did not fatigue himself, he said; on the contrary. He lived a Beethoven pause, he said, whatever he meant by that. In his anxiety to explain himself, he was liable to come to grief. Nay, this anxiety in itself, or so at least it seemed to me, constituted a breakdown in the self-sufficiency which he never wearied of arrogating to himself, a sorry collapse of my little internus homo, and alone sufficient to give him away as inept ape of his own shadow. But he wriggled out of everything by pleading that he had been drunk at the time, or that he was an incoherent person and content to remain so, and so on. He was an impossible person in the end. I gave him up in the end because he was not serious.

One day, in a positive geyser of confidence, he gave me an account of one of these 'moving pauses'. He had a strong weakness for oxymoron. In the same way he over-indulged in gin and tonic-water.

Not the least charm of this pure blank movement, this 'gress' or 'gression', was its aptness to receive, with or without the approval of the subject, in all their integrity the faint inscriptions of the outer world. Exempt from destination, it had not to shun the unforeseen nor turn aside from the agreeable odds and ends of vaudeville that

are liable to crop up. This sensitiveness was not the least charm of
this roaming that began by being blank, not the least charm of this
pure act the alacrity with which it welcomed defilement. But very
nearly the least.

Emerging, on the particular evening in question, from the underground convenience in the maw of College Street, with a vague
impression that he had come from following the sunset up the Liffey
till all the colour had been harried from the sky, all the tulips and
aerugo expunged, he squatted, not that he had too much drink
taken but simply that for the moment there were no grounds for his
favouring one direction rather than another, against Tommy
Moore's plinth. Yet he durst not dally. Was it not from brooding
shill I, shall I, dilly, dally, that he had come out? Now the summons
to move on was a subpoena. Yet he found he could not, any more
than Buridan's ass, move to right or left, backward or forward. Why
this was he could not make out at all. Nor was it the moment for
self-examination. He had experienced little or no trouble coming
back from the Park Gate along the north quay, he had taken the
Bridge and Westmoreland Street in his stride, and now he suddenly
found himself good for nothing but to loll against the plinth of this
bull-necked bard, and wait for a sign.

There were signs on all hands. There was the big Bovril sign to
begin with, flaring beyond the Green. But it was useless. Faith, Hope
and — what was it? — Love, Eden missed, every ebb derided, all the
tides ebbing from the shingle of Ego Maximus, little me. Itself it
went nowhere, only round and round, like the spheres, but mutely.
It could not dislodge him now, it could only put ideas into his head.
Was it not from sitting still among his ideas, other people's ideas,
that he had come away? What would he not give now to get on the
move again! Away from ideas!

Turning aside from this and other no less futile emblems, his
attention was arrested by a wheel-chair being pushed rapidly under
the arcade of the Bank, in the direction of Dame Street. It moved in
and out of sight behind the bars of the columns. This was the blind
paralytic who sat all day near to the corner of Fleet Street, and in
bad weather under the shelter of the arcade, the same being
wheeled home to his home in the Coombe. It was past his time and
there was a bitter look on his face. He would give his chairman a

piece of his mind when he got him to himself. This chairman, hireling or poor relation, came every evening a little before the dark, unfastened from the beggar's neck and breast the placard announcing his distress, tucked him up snugly in his coverings and wheeled him home to his supper. He was well advised to be assiduous, for this begger was a power in the Coombe. In the morning it was his duty to shave his man and wheel him, according to the weather, to one or other of his pitches. So it went, day after day.

This was a star the horizon adorning if you like, and Belacqua made off at all speed in the opposite direction. Down Pearse Street, that is to say, long straight Pearse Street, its vast Barrack of Glencullen granite, its home of tragedy restored and enlarged, its coal merchants and Florentine Fire Brigade Station, its two Cervi saloons, ice-cream and fried fish, its dairies, garages and monumental sculptors, and implicit behind the whole length of its southern frontage the College, Perpetuis futuris temporibus duraturum. It was to be hoped so, indeed.

It was a most pleasant street, despite its name, to be abroad in, full as it always was with shabby substance and honest-to-God coming and going. All day the roadway was a tumult of buses, red and blue and silver. By one of these a little girl was run down, just as Belacqua drew near to the railway viaduct. She had been to the Hibernian Dairies for milk and bread and then she had plunged out into the roadway, she was in such a childish fever to get back in record time with her treasure to the tenement in Mark Street where she lived. The good milk was all over the road and the loaf, which had sustained no injury, was sitting up against the kerb, for all the world as though a pair of hands had taken it up and set it down there. The queue standing for the Palace Cinema was torn between conflicting desires: to keep their places and to see the excitement. They craned their necks and called out to know the worst, but they stood firm. Only one girl, debauched in appearance and swathed in a black blanket, fell out near the sting of the queue and secured the loaf. With the loaf under her blanket she sidled unchallenged down Mark Street and turned into Mark Lane. When she got back to the queue her place had been taken of course. But her sally had not cost her more than a couple of yards.

Belacqua turned left into Lombard Street, the street of the sanitary engineers, and entered a public-house. Here he was known, in the sense that his grotesque exterior had long ceased to alienate the curates and make them giggle, and to the extent that he was served with his drink without having to call for it. This did not always seem a privilege. He was tolerated, what was more, and let alone by the rough but kindly habitués of the house, recruited for the most part from among dockers, railwaymen and vague joxers on the dole. Here also art and love, scrabbling in dispute or staggering home, were barred, or, perhaps better, unknown. The aesthetes and the impotent were far away.

These circumstances combined to make of this place a very grateful refuge for Belacqua, who never omitted, when he found himself in its neighbourhood with the price of a drink about him, to pay it a visit.

When I enquired how he squared such visits with his anxiety to keep on the move and his distress at finding himself brought to a standstill, as when he had come out of the underground in the mouth of College Street, he replied that he did not. 'Surely' he said 'my resolution has the right to break down.' I supposed so indeed. 'Or' he said 'if you prefer, I make the raid in two hops instead of non-stop. From what' he cried 'does that disqualify me, I should very much like to know.' I hastened to assure him that he had a perfect right to suit himself in what, after all, was a manoeuvre of his own contriving, and that the raid, to adopt his own term, lost nothing by being made in easy stages. 'Easy!' he exclaimed, 'how easy?'

But notice the double response, like two holes to a burrow.

Sitting in this crapulent den, drinking his drink, he gradually ceased to see its furnishings with pleasure, the bottles, representing centuries of loving research, the stools, the counter, the powerful screws, the shining phalanx of the pulls of the beer-engines, all cunningly devised and elaborated to further the relations between purveyor and consumer in this domain. The bottles drawn and emptied in a twinkling, the casks responding to the slightest pressure on their joysticks, the weary proletarians at rest on arse and elbow, the cash-register that never complains, the graceful curates flying from customer to customer, all this made up a spectacle in which Belacqua was used to take delight and chose to see a pleasant instance of machinery decently subservient to appetite. A great major symphony of supply and demand, effect and cause, fulcrate on the middle C of the counter and waxing, as it proceeded, in the charming harmonies of blasphemy and broken glass and all the aliquots of fatigue and ebriety. So that he would say that the only place where he could come to anchor and be happy was a low publichouse and that all the wearisome tactics of gress and dud Beethoven would be done away with if only he could spend his life in such a place. But as they closed at ten, and as residence and good faith were viewed as incompatible, and as in any case he had not the means to consecrate his life to stasis, even in the meanest bar, he supposed he must be content to indulge this whim from time to time, and return thanks for such sporadic mercy.

All this and much more he laboured to make clear. He seemed to derive considerable satisfaction from his failure to do so.

But on this particular occasion the cat failed to jump, with the result that he became as despondent as though he were sitting at home in his own great armchair, as anxious to get on the move and quite as hard put to it to do so. Why this was he could not make out. Whether the trituration of the child in Pearse Street had upset him without his knowing it, or whether (and he put forward this alternative with a truly insufferable complacency) he had come to some parting of the ways, he did not know at all. All he could say was that the objects in which he was used to find such recreation and repose lost gradually their hold upon him, he became insensible to them little by little, the old itch and algos crept back into his mind. He had come briskly all the way from Tommy Moore, and now he suddenly found himself sitting paralysed and grieving in a pub of all places, good for nothing but to stare at his spoiling porter and wait for a sign.

To this day he does not know what caused him to look up, but look up he did. Feeling the impulse to do this strong upon him, he forced his eyes away from the glass of dying porter and was rewarded by seeing a hatless woman advancing slowly towards him up the body of the bar. No sooner had she come in than he must have become aware of her. That was surely very curious in the first instance. She seemed to be hawking some ware or other, but what it was he could not see, except that it was not studs or laces or

matches or lavender or any of the usual articles. Not that it was
unusual to find a woman in that public-house, for they came and
went freely, slaking their thirst and beguiling their sorrows with no
less freedom than their menfolk. Indeed it was always a pleasure to
see them, their advances were always most friendly and honourable,
Belacqua had many a delightful recollection of their commerce.

Hence there was no earthly reason why he should see in the
advancing figure of this mysterious pedlar anything untoward, or in
the nature of the sign in default of which he was clamped to his
stool till closing-time. Yet the impulse to do so was so strong that
he yielded to it, and as she drew nearer, having met with more
rebuffs than pence in her endeavours to dispose of her wares, whatever they were, it became clear to him that his instinct had not
played him false, in so far at least as she was a woman of very
remarkable presence indeed.

Her speech was that of a woman of the people, but of a gentle-
woman of the people. Her gown had served its time, but yet contrived to be respectable. He noticed with a pang that she sported
about her neck the insidious little mock fur so prevalent in tony
slumland. The one deplorable feature of her get up, as apprehended
by Belacqua in his hasty survey, was the footwear – the cruel straight
outsizes of the suffragette or welfare worker. But he did not doubt
for a moment that they had been a gift, or picked up in the pop for
a song. She was of more than average height and well in flesh. She
might be past middle-age. But her face, ah her face, was what
Belacqua had rather refer to as her countenance, it was so full of
light. This she lifted up upon him and no error. Brimful of light and
serene, serenissime, it bore no trace of suffering, and in this alone
it might be said to be a notable face. Yet like tormented faces that
he had seen, like the face in the National Gallery in Merrion Square
by the Master of Tired Eyes, it seemed to have come a long way and
subtend an infinitely narrow angle of affliction, as eyes focus a star.
The features were null, only luminous, impassive and secure, petrified in radiance, or words to that effect, for the reader is requested
to take notice that this sweet style is Belacqua's. An act of expression, he said, a wreathing or wrinkling, could only have had the
effect of a dimmer on a headlight. The implications of this trium-
phant figure, the just and the unjust, etc., are better forgone.

At long last she addressed herself to Belacqua.

'Seats in heaven' she said in a white voice 'tuppence apiece, four fer a tanner.'

'No' said Belacqua. It was the first syllable to come to his lips. It had not been his intention to deny her.

'The best of seats' she said 'again I'm sold out. Tuppence apiece the best of seats, four fer a tanner.'

This was unforeseen with a vengeance, if not exactly vaudeville. Belacqua was embarrassed in the last degree, but transported also. He felt the sweat coming in the small of his back, above his Montrouge belt.

'Have you got them on you?' he mumbled.

'Heaven goes round' she said, whirling her arm, 'and round and round and round and round.'

'Yes,' said Belacqua 'round and round.'

'Rowan' she said, dropping the d's and getting more of a spin into the slogan, 'rowan an' rowan an' rowan.'

Belacqua scarcely knew where to look. Unable to blush he came out in this beastly sweat. Nothing of the kind had ever happened to him before. He was altogether disarmed, unsaddled and miserable. The eyes of them all, the dockers, the railwaymen and, most terrible of all, the joxers, were upon him. His tail drooped. This female dog of a pixy with her tiresome Ptolemy, he was at her mercy.

'No' he said 'no thank you, no not this evening thank you.'

'Again I'm sold out' she said 'an' buked out, four fer a tanner.'

'On whose authority . . .' began Belacqua, like a Scholar.

'For yer frien'' she said 'yer da, yer ma an' yer motte, four fer a tanner.' The voice ceased, but the face did not abate.

'How do I know' piped Belacqua 'you're not sellin' me a pup?'

'Heaven goes rowan an' rowan . . .'

'Rot you' said Belacqua 'I'll take two. How much is that?'

'Four dee' she said.

Belacqua gave her a sixpence.

'Gobbless yer honour' she said, in the same white voice from which she had not departed. She made to go.

'Here' cried Belacqua 'you owe me twopence.' He had not even the good grace to say tuppence.

'Arragowan' she said 'make it four cantcher, yer frien', yer da, yer ma an' yer motte.'

Belacqua could not bicker. He had not the strength of mind for that. He turned away.

'Jesus' she said distinctly 'and his sweet mother preserve yer honour.'

'Amen' said Belacqua, into his dead porter.

Now the woman went away and her countenance lighted her to her room in Townsend Street.

But Belacqua tarried a little to listen to the music. Then he also departed, but for Railway Street, beyond the river.

A WET NIGHT

HARK, IT IS the season of festivity and goodwill. Shopping is in full swing, the streets are thronged with revellers, the Corporation has offered a prize for the best-dressed window, Hyam's trousers are down again.

Mistinguett would do away with chalets of necessity. She does not think them necessary. Not so Belacqua. Emerging happy body from the hot bowels of McLoughlin's he looked up and admired the fitness of Moore's bull neck, not a whit too short, with all due respect to the critics. Bright and cheery above the strom of the Green, as though coached by the Star of Bethlehem, the Bovril sign danced and danced through its seven phases.

The lemon of faith jaundiced, annunciating the series, was in a fungus of hopeless green reduced to shingles and abolished. Whereupon the light went out, in homage to the slain. A sly ooze of gules, carmine of solicitation, lifting the skirts of green that the prophecy might be fulfilled, shocking Gabriel into cherry, flooded the sign. But the long skirts came rattling down, darkness covered their shame, the cycle was at an end. Da capo.

Bovril into Salome, thought Belacqua, and Tommy Moore there with his head on his shoulders. Doubt, Despair and Scrounging, shall I hitch my bath-chair to the greatest of these? Across the way, beneath the arcade, the blind paralytic was in position, he was well tucked up in his coverings, he was lashing into his dinner like any proletarian. Soon his man would come and wheel him home. No one had ever seen him come or go, he was there one minute and gone the next. He went and returned. When you scrounge you must go and return, that was the first great article of Christian scrounging. No man could settle down to scrounge properly in a foreign land. The Wanderjahre were a sleep and a forgetting, the proud dead point. You came back wise and staked your best in some sheltered place, pennies trickled in, you were looked up to in a tenement.

Belacqua had been proffered a sign, Bovril had made him a sign.

Whither next? To what licensed premises? To where the porter was well up, first; and the solitary shawly like a cloud of latter rain in a waste of poets and politicians, second; and he neither knew nor was known, third. A lowly house dear to shawlies where the porter was up and he could keep himself to himself on a high stool with a high round and feign to be immersed in the Moscow notes of the Twilight Herald. These were very piquant.

Of the two houses that appealed spontaneously to these exigencies the one, situate in Merrion Row, was a home from home for jarveys. As some folk from hens, so Belacqua shrank from jarveys. Rough, gritty, almost verminous men. From Moore to Merrion Row, moreover, was a perilous way, beset at this hour with poets and peasants and politicians. The other lay in Lincoln Place, he might go gently by Pearse Street, there was nothing to stop him. Long straight Pearse Street, it permitted of a simple cantilena in his mind, its footway peopled with the tranquil and detached in fatigue, its highway dehumanised in a tumult of buses. Trams were monsters, moaning along beneath the wild gesture of the trolley. But buses were pleasant, tyres and glass and clash and no more. Then to pass by the Queens, home of tragedy, was charming at that hour, to pass between the old theatre and the long line of the poor and lowly queued up for thruppence worth of pictures. For there Florence would slip into the song, the Piazza della Signoria and the No 1 tram and the Feast of St John, when they lit the torches of resin on the towers and the children, while the rockets at nightfall above the Cascine were still flagrant in their memory, opened the little cages to the glutted cicadae after their long confinement and stayed out with their young parents long after their usual bedtime. Then slowly in his mind down the sinister Uffizi to the parapets of Arno, and so on and so forth. This pleasure was dispensed by the Fire Station opposite which seemed to have been copied here and there from the Palazzo Vecchio. In deference to Savonarola? Ha! ha! At all events it was as good a way as any other to consume the Homer hour, darkness filling the streets and so on, and a better than most in virtue of his great thirst towards the lowly house that would snatch him in off the street through the door of its grocery department if by good fortune that were still open.

Painfully then under the College ramparts, past the smart taxis, he set off, clearing his mind for its song. The Fire Station worked without a hitch and all was going as well as could be expected considering what the evening held in pickle for him when the blow fell. He was run plump into by one Chas, a highbrow bromide of French nationality with a diabolical countenance compound of Skeat's and Paganini's and a mind like a tattered concordance. It was Chas who would not or could not leave well alone, Belacqua being rapt in his burning feet and the line of the song in his head.

'Halte-là' piped the pirate, 'wither so gay?'

In the lee of the Monumental Showroom Belacqua was obliged to pause and face this machine. It carried butter and eggs from the Hibernian Dairy. Belacqua however was not to be drawn.

'Ramble,' he said vaguely 'in the twilight.'

'Just a song' said Chas 'at twilight. No?'

Belacqua tormented his hands in the gloom. Had he been blocked on his way and violated in the murmur of his mind to listen to this clockwork Bartlett? Apparently.

'How's the world' he said nevertheless, in spite of everything, 'and what's the news of the great world?'

'Fair' said Chas, cautiously, 'fair to meedling. The poem moves, eppure.'

If he mentions ars longa, Belacqua made this covenant with himself, he will have occasion to regret it.

'Limae labor' said Chas 'et mora.'

'Well' said Belacqua, casting off with clean hands, 'see you again.'

'But shortly, I thrrust' cried Chas, 'Casa Frica, di collied night. No?'

'Alas' said Belacqua, well adrift.

Behold the Frica, she visits talent in the Service Flats. In she lands, singing Havelock Ellis in a deep voice, frankly itching to work that which is not seemly. Open upon her concave breast as on a lectern lies Portigliotti's Penombre Claustrali, bound in tawed caul. In her talons earnestly she grasps Sade's 120 Days and the Anterotica of Aliosha G. Brignole-Sale, unopened, bound in shagreened caul. A septic pudding hoodwinks her, a stodgy turban of pain it laps her horse face. The eyehole is clogged with the bulbus, the round pale globe goggles exposed. Solitary meditation has furnished her with nostrils of generous bore. The mouth champs an invisible bit, foam gathers at the bitter commissures. The crateriform brisket, lipped with sills of paunch, cowers ironically behind a maternity tunic. Keyholes have wrung the unfriendly withers, the osseous rump screams behind the hobble-skirt. Wastes of woad worsted advertise the pasterns. Aïe!

This in its absinthe whinny had bidden Belacqua and, what is more, the Alba, to backstairs, claret cup and the intelligentsia. The Alba, Belacqua's current one and only, had much pleasure in accepting for her scarlet gown and broad pale bored face. The belle of the ball. Aïe!

But seldom one without two and scarcely had Chas been shed than lo from out the Grosvenor sprang the homespun Poet wiping his mouth and a little saprophile of an anonymous politico-ploughboy setting him off. The Poet sucked his teeth over this unexpected pleasure. The golden eastern lay of his bullet head was muted by no covering. Beneath the Wally Whitmaneen of his Donegal tweeds a body was to be presumed. He gave the impression of having lost a harrow and found a figure of speech. Belacqua was numbed.

'Drink' decreed the Poet in a voice of thunder.

Belacqua slunk at his heels into the Grosvenor, the gimlet eyes of the saprophile probed his loins.

'Now' exulted the Poet, as though he had just brought an army across the Beresina, 'give it a name and knock it back.'

'Pardon me' stuttered Belacqua 'just a moment, will you be so kind.' He waddled out of the bar and into the street and up it at all speed and into the lowly public through the groceries door like a bit of dirt into a Hoover. This was a rude thing to do. When intimidated he was rude beyond measure, not timidly insolent like Stendhal's Comte de Thaler, but finally rude on the sly. Timidly insolent when, as by Chas, exasperated; finally rude on the sly when intimidated, outrageously rude behind the back of his oppressor. This was one of his little peculiarities.

He bought a paper of a charming little sloven, no but a truly exquisite little page, a freelance clearly, he would not menace him, he skipped in on his miry bare feet with only three or four under his oxter for sale. Belacqua gave him a thruppenny bit and a cigarette picture. He sat to himself on a stool in the central leaf of the main triptych, his feet on a round so high that his knees topped the curb of the counter (admirable posture for a man with a weak bladder and tendency to ptosis of viscera), drank despondent porter (but he dared not budge) and devoured the paper.

'A woman' he read with a thrill 'is either: a short-below-the-waist, a big-hip, a sway-back, a big-abdomen or an average. If the bust be too cogently controlled, then shall fat roll from scapula to scapula. If it be made passable and slight, then shall the diaphragm bulge and be unsightly. Why not therefore invest chez a reputable corset-builder in the brassière-cum-corset décolleté, made from the finest Broches, Coutils and Elastics, centuple stitched in wearing parts, fitted with immovable spiral steels? It bestows stupendous diaphragm and hip support, it enhances the sleeveless backless neckless evening gown ...'

O Love! O Fire! but would the scarlet gown lack all these parts? Was she a short-below or a sway-back? She had no waist, nor did she deign to sway. She was not to be classified. Not to be corseted. Not woman of flesh.

The face on the curate faded away and Grock's appeared in its stead.

'Say that again' said the red gash in the white putty.

Belacqua said it all and much more.

'Nisscht mööööööglich' moaned Grock, and was gone.

Now Belacqua began to worry lest the worst should come to the worst and the scarlet gown be backless after all. Not that he had any doubts as to the back thus bared being a sight for sore eyes. The omoplates would be well defined, they would have a fine free ball-and-socket motion. In repose they would be the blades of an anchor, the delicate furrow of the spine its stem. His mind pored over this back that inspired him with awe. He saw it as a flower-de-luce, a spatulate leaf with segments angled back, like the wings of a butterfly sucking a blossom, from their common hinge. Then fetching from further afield, as an obelisk, a cross-potent, pain and death, still death, a bird crucified on a wall. This flesh and bones swathed in scarlet, this heart of washed flesh draped in scarlet ...

Unable to bear any longer his doubts as to the rig of the gown he passed through the counter and got her house on the telephone.

'Dressing' said the maid, the Venerilla, his friend and bawd to be, 'and spitting blood.'

No, she could not be got down, she had been up in her room cursing and swearing for the past hour.

'I'm afeared of me gizzard' said the voice 'to go near her.'

'Is it closed at the back' demanded Belacqua 'or is it open?'

'Is what?'

'The gown' cried Belacqua, 'what else? Is it closed?'

The Venerilla requested him to hold on while she called it to the eye of the mind. The objurgations of this ineffiable member were clearly audible.

'Would it be the red one?' she said, after countless ages.

'The scarlet bloody gown of course' he cried out of his torment, 'do you not know?'

'Hold on now . . . It buttons . . .'

'Buttons? What buttons?'

'It buttons ups behind, sir, with the help of God.'

'Say it again' implored Belacqua, 'over and over again.'

'Amn't I after saying' groaned the Venerilla 'it buttons ups on her.'

'Praise be to God' said Belacqua 'and his blissful Mother.'

Calm now and sullen the Alba, dressed insidiously up to the nines, bides her time in the sunken kitchen, paying no heed to her foot and foil who has made bold to lay open Belacqua's distress. She is in pain, her brandy is at hand, mulling in the big glass on the range. Behind her frontage abandoned in elegance, sagging in its elegance and clouded in its native sorrow, a more anxious rite than sumptuous meditation is in progress. For her mind is at prayer-stool before a perhaps futile purpose, she is loading the spring of her mind for a perhaps unimportant undertaking. Letting her outside rip pro tem, she is screwing herself up and up, she is winding up the weights of her mind, to being the belle of the ball, banquet or party. Any less beautiful girl would have contemned such tactics and considered this class of absorption at the service of so simple an occasion unwarranted and, what was worse, a sad give away. Here am I, a less bountiful one would have argued, the belle, and there is the ball; let these two items be brought together and the thing is done. Are we then to insinuate, with such a simplist, that the Alba questioned the virtue of her appearance. Indeed and indeed we are not. She had merely to unleash her eyes, she had merely to unhood them, as well she knew, and she might have mercy on whom she would. There was no difficulty about that. But what she did question, balefully, as though she knew the answer in advance, was the fitness of a distinction hers for the asking, of a palm that she had merely to open her eyes and assume. That the simplicity of the gest turned her in the first place against it, relegating it among the multitude of things that were not her genre, is indisputable. But this was only a minute aspect of her position. It is with the disparagement attaching in the thought of Belacqua, and in hers tending to, to the quality of the exploit that she now wrestles. It is with its no doubt unworthiness that she now has to do. Sullen and still, aware of the brandy at hand but not thirsting for it, she cranks herself up to a reality of preference, slowly but surely she gilds her option, she exalts it into realms of choice. She will do this thing, she will, she will be belle of the ball, gladly, gravely and carefully, humiliter, fideliter, simpliciter, and not merely because she might just as well. Is she, she a woman of the world, she who knows, to halt between two opinions, founder in a strait of two wills, hang in suspense and be the more killed? She who knows? So far from such nonsense she will soon chafe to be off. And now she dare, until it be time, the clock strike, delegate a portion of her attention with instructions to reorganise her features, hands, shoulders, back, outside in a world, the inside having been spiked. At once she thirsts for the Hennessy. She sings to herself, for her own pleasure, stressing all the words that cry for stress, like Dan the first to warble without fear or favour:

> No me jodas en el suelo
> Como si fuera una perra,
> Que con esos cojonazos
> Me echas en el cono tierra.

The Polar Bear, a big old brilliant lecher, was already on his way, speeding along the dark dripping country roads in a crass honest slob of a clangorous bus, engaging with the effervescent distinction of a Renaissance cardinal in rather languid tongue-play an acquaintance of long standing, a Jesuit with little or no nonsense about him.

'The Lebensbahn' he was saying, for he never used the English word when the foreign pleased him better, 'of the Galilean is the tragi-comedy of the solipsism that will not capitulate. The humilities and retro me's and quaffs of sirreverence are on a par with the hey presto's, arrogance and egoism. He is the first great self-contained playboy. The cryptic abasement before the woman taken red-handed is as great a piece of megalomaniacal impertinence as his interference in the affairs of his boy-friend Lazarus. He opens the series of slick suicides, as opposed to the serious Empedoclean variety. He has to answer for the wretched Nemo and his coratés, bleeding in paroxysms of dépit on an unimpressed public.'

He coughed up a plump cud of mucus, spun it round the avid bowl of his palate and stowed it away for future degustation.

The S.J. with little or no nonsense had just enough strength to voice his fatigue.

'If you knew' he said 'how you bore me with your twice two is four.'

The P.B. failed to get him.

'You bore me' drawled the S.J. 'worse than an infant prodigy.' He paused to recruit his energies. 'In his hairless voice' he proceeded 'preferring the druggist Borodine to Mozart.'

'By all accounts' retorted the P.B. 'your sweet Mozart was a Hexenmeister in the pilch.'

That was a nasty one, let him make what he liked of that one.

'Our Lord—'

'Speak for yourself' said the P.B., nettled beyond endurance.

'Our Lord was not.'

'You forget,' said the P.B., 'he got it all over at procreation.'

'When you grow up to be a big boy' said the Jesuit 'and can understand the humility that is beyond masochism, come and talk to me again. Not cis-, ultra-masochistic. Beyond pain and service.'

'But precisely' exclaimed the P.B., 'he did not serve, the late lamented. What else am I saying? A valet does not have big ideas. He let down the central agency.'

'The humility' murmured the janizary 'of a love too great for skivvying and too real to need the tonic of urtication.'

The infant prodigy sneered at this comfortable variety.

'You make things pleasant for yourselves' he sneered, 'I must say.'

'The best reason' said the S.J. 'that can be given for believing is that it is more amusing. Disbelief' said the soldier of Christ, making ready to arise 'is a bore. We do not count our change. We simply cannot bear to be bored.'

'Say that from the pulpit' said the P.B. 'and you'll be drummed into the wilderness.'

The S.J. laughed profusely. Was it possible to conceive a more artless impostor of a mathematician than this fellow!

'Would you' he begged, putting his greatcoat on, 'would you, my dear good fellow, have the kindness to bear in mind that I am not a Parish Priest.'

'I won't forget' said the P.B. 'that you don't scavenge. Your love is too great for the slops.'

'Egg-sactly' said the S.J. 'But they are excellent men. A shade on the assiduous side, a shade too anxious to strike a rate. Otherwise . . .' He rose. 'Observe' he said, 'I desire to get down. I pull this cord and the bus stops and lets me down.'

The P.B. observed.

'In just such a Gehenna of links' said this remarkable man, with one foot on the pavement, 'I forged my vocation.'

With which words he was gone and the burden of his fare had fallen on the P.B.

Chas's girl was a Shetland Shawly. He had promised to pick her up on his way to Casa Frica and now, cinched beyond reproach in his double-breasted smoking, he subdued his impatience to catch a tram in order to explain the world to a group of students.

'The difference, if I may say so—'

'Oh' cried the students, una voce, 'oh please!'

'The difference, then, I say, between Bergson and Einstein, the essential difference, is as between philosopher and sociolog.'

'Oh!' cried the students.

'Yes' said Chas, casting up what was the longest divulgation he could place before the tram, which had hove into view, would draw abreast.

'And if it is the smart thing now to speak of Bergson as a cod' — he edged away — 'it is that we move from the Object' — he made a plunge for the tram — 'and the Idea to SENSE' — he cried from the step — 'AND REASON.'

'Sense' echoed the students 'and reason!'

The difficulty was to know what exactly he meant by sense.

'He must mean senses' said a first, 'smell, don't you know, and so on.'

'Nay,' said a second, 'he must mean common sense.'

'I think' said a third, 'he must mean instinct, intuition, don't you know, and that kind of thing.'

A fourth longed to know what Object there was in Bergson, a fifth what a sociolog was, a sixth what either had to do with the world.

'We must ask him' said a seventh, 'that is all. We must not confuse ourselves with inexpert speculation. Then we shall see who is right.'

'We must ask him' cried the students, 'then we shall see . . .'

On which understanding, that the first to see him again would be sure and ask him, they went their not so very different ways.

The hair of the homespun Poet, so closely was it cropped, did not lend itself kindly to any striking effects of dressing. Here again, in his plumping for the austerity of a rat's back, he proclaimed himself in reaction to the nineties. But the little that there was to do he had done, with a lotion that he had he had given alertness to the stubble. Also he had changed his tie and turned his collar. And now, though alone and unobserved, he paced up and down. He was making up his piece, d'occasion perhaps in both senses, whose main features he had recently established riding home on his bike from the Yellow House. He would deliver it when his hostess came with her petition, he would not hum and haw like an amateur pianist nor yet as good as spit in her eye like a professional one. No, he would arise and say, not declaim, state gravely, with the penetrating Middle West gravity that is like an ogleful of tears:

Calvary by Night

the water
the waste of water

in the womb of water
an pansy leaps.

rocket of bloom flare flower of night wilt for me
on the breasts of the water it has closed it has made
an act of floral presence on the water
the tranquil act of its cycle on the waste
from the spouting forth
to the re-enwombing
untroubled bow of petaline sweet-smellingness
kingfisher abated
drowned for me
lamb of insustenance mine

till the clamour of a blue bloom
beat on the walls of the womb of
the waste of
the water

Resolved to put across this strong composition and cause something of a flutter he was anxious that there should be no flaw in the mode of presentation adopted by him as most worthy of his aquatic manner. In fact he had to have it pat in order not to have to say it pat, in order to give the impression that in the travail of its exteriorisation he was being torn asunder. Taking his cue from the equilibrist, who enraptures us by failing once, twice, three times, and then, in a regular lather of volition, bringing it off, he deemed that this little turn, if it were to conquer the salon, required stress to be laid not so much on the content of the performance as on the spiritual evisceration of the performer. Hence he paced to and fro, making a habit of the words and effects of Calvary by Night.

The Frica combed her hair, back and back she raked her purple tresses till to close her eyes became a problem. The effect was throttled gazelle, more appropriate to evening wear than her workaday foal at foot. Belacqua's Ruby, in her earlier campaigns, had favoured the same taut Sabine coiffure, till Mrs Tough, by dint of protesting that it made her little bird-face look like a sucked lozenge, had induced her to fluff things a bit and crimp them. Unavailingly alas! for nimbed she was altogether too big dolly that opens and shuts its eyes. Nor indeed was lozenge, sucked or buck, by any means the most ignoble office that face of woman might discharge. For here at hand, saving us our fare to Derbyshire, we have the Frica, looking something horrid.

Throttled gazelle gives no idea. Her features, as though the hand of an unattractive ravisher were knotted in her chevelure, were set at half-cock and locked in a rictus. She had frowned to pencil her eyebrows, so now she had four. The dazzled iris was domed in a white agony of entreaty, the upper-lip writhed back in a snarl to the untented nostrils. Would she bite her tongue off, that was the interesting question. The nutcracker chin betrayed a patent clot of thyroid gristle. It was impossible to set aside the awful suspicion that her flattened mammae, in sympathy with this tormented eructation of countenance, had put forth cutwaters and were rowelling her corsage. But the face was beyond appeal, a flagrant seat of injury. She had merely to arrange her hands so that the palm and fingers of the one touched the palm and fingers of the other and hold them thus joined before the breast with a slight upward inclination to look like a briefless martyress in rut.

Nevertheless the arty Countess of Parabimbi, backing through the press, would dangle into the mauve presence of the crone-mother, Caleken Frica's holiest thing alive, and

'My dear' she would positively be obliged to ejaculate, 'never have I seen your Caleken quite so striking! Simply Sistine!'

What would her Ladyship be pleased to mean? The Cumaean Sibyl on a bearing-rein, sniffing the breeze for the Grimm Brothers? Oh, her Ladyship did not care to be so infernal finical and nice, that would be like working out how many pebbles in Tom Thumb's pocket. It was just a vague impression, it was merely that she looked, with that strange limey hobnailed texture of complexion, so frescosa, from the waist up, my dear, with that distempered cobalt modesty-piece, a positive gem of ravished Quattrocento, a positive jewel, my dear, of sweaty Big Tom. Whereupon the vidual virgin, well aware after these many years that all things in heaven, the earth and the waters were as they were taken, would vow to cherish as long as she was spared the learned praise of such an expert.

'Maaaacche!' bleats the Parabimbi.

This may be premature. We have set it down too soon, perhaps. Still, let it bloody well stand.

To return to the Frica, there is the bell at long last, pealing down her Fallopian pipettes, galvanising her away from the mirror as though her navel had been pressed in annunciation.

The Student, whose name we shall never know, was the first to arrive. A foul little brute he was, with a brow.

'Oh Lawdee!' he gushed, his big brown eyes looking della Robbia babies at the Frica, 'don't tell me I'm the first!'

'Don't distress yourself' said Caleken, who could smell a poet against the wind, 'only by a short gaffe.'

Hard on the heels of the Poet came a gaggle of nondescripts, then a public botanist, then a Galway Gael, then the Shetland Shawly with her Chas. Him the Student, mindful of his pledge, accosted.

'In what sense' — he would have it out of him or perish — 'did you use sense when you said . . . ?'

'He said that?' exclaimed the botanist.

'Chas' said Caleken, as though she were announcing the name of a winner.

'Adsum' admitted Chas.

A plum of phlegm burst in the vestibule.

'What I want to know' complained the Student, 'what we all want to know, is in what sense he was using sense when he said . . .'

The Gael, in the heart of a cabbage of nondescripts, was bungling Duke Street's thought for the day to the crone.

'Owen . . .' he began again, when a nameless ignoramus, anxious to come into the picture as early on in the proceedings as possible, said rashly:

'What Owen?'

'Good evening' squalled the Polar Bear, 'good evening good evening good evening. Wat a night, Madame' he addressed himself vehemently, out of sheer politeness, directly to his hostess, 'God! wat a night!'

The crone was as fond of the P.B. as though she had bought him in Clery's toy fair.

'And you so far to come!' She wished she could dandle him on her knee. He was a shabby man and often moody. 'Too good of you to come' she hushabied, 'too good of you.'

The Man of Law, his face a blaze of acne, was next, escorting the Parabimbi and three tarts dressed for the backstairs.

'I met him' whispered Chas 'zigzagging down Pearse Street, Brunswick Street, you know, that was.'

'En route?' ventured Caleken. She was a bit above herself with all the excitment.

'Hein?'

'On his way here?'

'Well' said Chas, 'I regret, my dear Miss Frica, that he did not make it absolutely clear if he comes or not.'

The Gael said to the P.B. in an injured voice:

'Here's a man who wants to know what Owen.'

'Not possible' said the P.B., 'you astonish me.'

'Is it of the sweet mouth?' said a sandy son of Ham.

Now the prong of the P.B.'s judgment was keen and bright.

'That emmerdeur' he jeered, 'the strange sweet mouth!'

The Parabimbi jumped.

'You said?' she said.

Caleken emerged from the ruck, she came to the fore.

'What can be keeping the girls' she said. It was not exactly a question.

'And your sister' enquired the botanist, 'your charming sister, where can she be this evening now I wonder.'

The Beldam sprang into the breach.

'Unfortunately' she said, in ringing tones and with great precipitation, 'in bed, unwell. A great disappointment to us all.'

'Thank you, no. Happily not. A slight indisposition. Poor little Dandelion.' The Beldam heaved a heavy sigh.

The P.B. exchanged a look of intelligence with the Gael.

'What girls?' he said.

Caleken expanded her lungs:

'Pansy' – the Poet had a palpitation, why had he not brought his nux vomica? – 'Lilly Neary, Olga, Elliseva, Bride Maria, Alga, Ariana, tall Tib, slender Sib, Alma Beatrix, Alba—' They were really too numerous, she could not go through the entire list. She staunched her mouth.

'Alba!' ejaculated the P.B., 'Alba! She!'

'And why' interposed the Countess of Parabimbi 'why not Alba, whoever she may be, rather than, say, the Wife of Bath?'

A nondescript appeared in their midst, he panted the glad tidings. The girls had arrived.

'They are gurrls' said the botanist 'beyond question. But are they *the* gurrls?'

'Now I hope we can start' said the younger Frica, and, the elder being aware of no let or hindance, up on to the estrade smartly she stepped and unveiled the refreshments. Turning her back on the high dumb-waiter, with a great winged gesture of lapidated piety, she instituted the following selection:

'Cup! Squash! Cocoa! Force! Julienne! Pan Kail! Cock-a-Leekie! Hulluah! Apfelmus! Isinglass! Ching-Ching!'

A terrible silence fell on the assembly.

'Great cry' said Chas 'and little wool.'

The more famished faithful stormed the platform.

Two banned novelists, a bibliomaniac and his mistress, a paleographer, a violist d'amore with his instrument in a bag, a popular parodist with his sister and six daughters, a still more popular Professor of Bullscrit and Comparative Ovoidology, the saprophile the better for drink, a communist painter and decorator fresh back from the Moscow reserves, a merchant prince, two grave Jews, a rising strumpet, three more poets with Lauras to match, a disaffected cicisbeo, a chorus of playwrights, the inevitable envoy of the Fourth Estate, a phalanx of Grafton Street Stürmers and Jemmy Higgins arrived now in a body. No sooner had they been absorbed than the Parabimbi, very much the lone bird on this occasion in the absence of her husband the Count who had been unable to escort her on account of his being buggered if he would, got in her attributions of the Frica for which, as has been shown, the Beldam was so profoundly beholden.

'Maaaacche!' said the Countess of Parabimbi, 'I do but constate.'

She held the saucer under her chin like a communion-card. She lowered the cup into its socket without a sound.

'Excellent' she said, 'most excellent Force.'

The crone smiled from the teeth outward.

'So glad' she said, 'so glad.'

The Professor of Bullscrit and Comparative Ovoidology was no-where to be seen. But that was not his vocation, he was not a little boy. His function was to be heard. He was widely and distinctly heard.

'When the immortal Byron' he bombled 'was about to leave Ravenna, to sail in search of some distant shore where a hero's death might end his immortal spleen . . .'

'Ravenna!' exclaimed the Countess, memory tugging at her care-fully cultivated heart-strings, 'did I hear someone say Ravenna?'

'Allow me' said the rising strumpet: 'a sandwich: egg, tomato, cucumber.'

'Did you know' blundered the Man of Law 'that the Swedes have no fewer than seventy varieties of Smoerrbroed?'

The voice of the arithmomaniac was heard:

'The arc' he said, stooping to all in the great plainness of his words, 'is longer than its chord.'

'Madam knows Ravenna?' said the paleographer.

'Do I know Ravenna!' exclaimed the Parabimbi. 'Sure I know Ravenna. A sweet and noble city.'

'You know of course' said the Man of Law 'that Dante died there.'

'Right' said the Parabimbi, 'so he did.'

'You know of course' said the Professor 'that his tomb is in the Piazza Byron. I did his epitaph in the eye into blank heroics.'

'You know of course' said the paleographer 'that under Beli-sarius . . .'

'My dear' said the Parabimbi to the Beldam, 'how well it goes. What a happy party and how at home they all seem. I declare' she declared 'I envy you your flair for making people feel at their ease.'

The Beldam disclaimed faintly any such faculty. It was Caleken's party reelly, it was Caleken who had arranged everything reelly. She personally had had very little to do with the arrangements. She just sat there and looked exhausted. She was just a weary old Norn.

'To my thinking' boomed the Professor, begging the question as usual, 'the greatest triumph of the human mind was the calculation of Neptune from the observed vagaries of the orbit of Uranus.'

'And yours' said the P.B. That was an apple of gold and a picture of silver if you like.

The Parabimbi waxed stiff.

'What's that?' she cried, 'what's that he says?'

A still more terrible silence fell on the assembly. The saprophile had slapped the communist painter and decorator.

The Frica, supported by Mr Higgins, pounced on the disturbance.

'Go' she said to the saprophile 'and let there be no scene.'

Mr Higgins, who kicked up his heels in the scrum for the Rangers, made short work of the nuisance. The Frica turned on the poor P. and D.

'It is not my intention' she said 'to tolerate hooligans in this house.'

'He called me a bloody Bolshy' protested the glorious Komsomolet, 'and he a labour man himself.'

'Let there be no more of it' said the Frica, 'let there be no more of it.' She was very optative. 'I beg of you.' She stepped back fleetly to the altar.

'You heard what she said' said the Gael.

'Let there be no more of it' said the native speaker.

'I beg of you' said the P.B.

But now she cometh that all this may disdain, Alba, dauntless daughter of desires. Entering just on the turn of the hush, advancing like a midinette to pay her ironical respects to the Beldam, she fired the thorns under every pot. Turning her scarlet back on the crass crackling of the Parabimbi she mounted the estrade and there, silent and still before the elements of refreshment, in profile to the assistance, cast her gravitational nets.

The rising strumpet studied how to do it. The sister of the parodist passed on to such as were curious what little she and her dear nieces knew of the Alba who was much spoken of in certain virtuous circles to which they had access, though to be sure how much of what they heard was true and how much mere idle gossip they were really not in a position to determine. However, for what it was worth, it appeared ...

The Gael, the native speaker, a space-writer and the violist d'amore got together as though by magic.

'Well' invited the space-writer.

'Pret-ty good' said the Gael.

'Ex-quisite' said the violist d'amore.

The native speaker said nothing.

'Well' insisted the space-writer, 'Larry?'

Larry tore his eyes away from the estrade and said, drawing his palms slowly up the flanks of his kilt:

'Jaysus!'

'Meaning to say?' said the space-writer.

Larry turned his wild gaze back on the estrade.

'You don't happen to know' he said finally 'does she?'

'They all do' said the violist d'amore.

'Like hell they do' groaned the Gael, ricordandosi del tempo felice.

'What I want to know' said the Student, 'what we all are most anxious to know . . .'

'Some do abstain' said the space-writer, 'our friend here is right, through bashfulness from venery. It is a pity, but there you are.'

Great wits will jump and Jemmy Higgins and the P.B. converged on the estrade.

'You look pale' said the Frica 'and ill, my pet.'

The Alba raised her big head from the board, looked longly at the Frica, closed her eyes and intoned:

> Woe and Pain, Pain and Woe,
> Are my lot, night and noon . .

Caleken fell back.

'Keep them off' said the Alba.

'Keep them off!' echoed Caleken, 'keep them off?'

'We go through this world' observed the Alba 'like sunbeams through cracks in cucumbers.'

Caleken was not so sure about the sunbeams.

'Take a little cup' she urged, 'it will do you good. Or a Ching-Ching.'

'Keep them off' said the Alba, 'off off off off.'

But the P.B. and Higgins were on the estrade, they hemmed her in.

'So be it' said the Alba, 'let it run over by all means.'

Phew! The Frica was unspeakably relieved.

Half-past nine. The guests, led by the rising strumpet and declining cicisbeo, began to scatter through the house. The Frica let them go. In due course she would visit the alcoves, she would round them up for the party proper to begin. Had not Chas promised a piece of old French? Had not the Poet written a poem specially? She had peeped into the bag in the hall and seen the viol d'amore. So they would have a little music.

Half-past nine. It was raining bitterly when Belacqua, keyed up to take his bearings, issued forth into the unintelligible world of Lincoln Place. But he had bought a bottle, it was like a breast in the pocket of his reefer. He set off unsteadily by the Dental Hospital. As a child he had dreaded its façade, its sheets of blood-red glass. Now they were black, which was worse again, he having put aside a childish thing or two. Feeling suddenly white and clammy he leaned against the iron wicket set in the College wall and looked at Johnston, Mooney and O'Brien's clocks. Something to ten by the whirligig and he disinclined to stand, let alone walk. And the daggers of rain. He raised his hands and held them before his face, so close that even in the dark he could see the lines. They smelt bad. He carried them on to his forehead, the fingers sank in his wet hair, the heels crushed torrents of indigo out of his eyeballs, the rabbet of his nape took the cornice, it wrung the baby anthrax that he always wore just above his collar, he intensified the pressure and the pangs, they were a guarantee of identity.

The next thing was his hands dragged roughly down from his eyes, which he opened on the vast crimson face of an ogre. For a moment it was still, plush gargoyle, then it moved, it was convulsed. This, he thought, is the face of some person talking. It was. It was that part of a Civic Guard pouring abuse upon him. Belacqua closed his eyes, there was no other way of ceasing to see it. Subduing a great desire to visit the pavement he catted, with undemonstrative abundance, all over the boots and trouser-ends of the Guard, in return for which incontinence he received such a dunch on the breast that he fell hip and thigh into the outskirts of his own offal. He had no feeling of hurt either to his person or to his amour propre, only a very amiable weakness and an impatience to be on the move. It must have gone ten. He bore no animosity towards the Guard, although now he began to hear what he was saying. He knelt before him in the filth, he heard all the odious words he was saying in the recreation of his duty and bore him not the slightest ill-will. He reached up for a purchase on his gleaming cape and hoisted himself to his feet. The apology he made when stable for what had occured was profusely rejected. He furnished his name and address, whence he came and whither he went, and why, his occupation and immediate business, and why. It distressed him to learn that for two pins the Guard would frog-march him to the Station, but he appreciated the officer's dilemma.

'Wipe them boots' said the Guard.

Belacqua was only too happy, it was the least he could do. Contriving two loose swabs of the Twilight Herald he stooped and cleaned the boots and trouser-ends to the best of his ability. A magnificent and enormous pair of boots emerged. He rose, clutching the fouled swabs, and looked up timidly at the Guard, who seemed rather at a loss as how best to press home his advantage.

'I trust, Sergeant,' said Belacqua, in a murmur pitched to melt the hardest heart, 'that you can see your way to overlooking my misdemeanour.'

Justice and mercy had doubtless joined their ancient issues in the conscience of the Guard, for he said nothing. Belacqua tendered his right hand, innocent of any more mercantile commodity than that 'gentle peace' recommended by the immortal Shakespeare, having first wiped it clean on his sleeve. This member the Dogberry, after a brief converse with his incorruptible heart, was kind enough to invest with the office of a cuspidor. Belacqua strangled a shrug and moved away in a tentative manner.

'Hold on there' said the Guard.

Belacqua halted, but in a very irritating way, as though he had just remembered something. The Guard, who had much more of the lion than of the fox, kept him standing until inside his helmet the throbbing of his Leix and Offaly head became more than he could endure. He then decided to conclude his handling of this small affair of public order.

'Move on' he said.

Belacqua walked away, holding tightly on to the swabs, which he rightly interpreted as litter. Once safely round the corner of Kildare Street he let them fall. Then after a few paces forward, he halted, turned, hastened back to where they were fidgeting on the pavement and threw them into an area. Now he felt extraordinarily light and limber and haeres caeli. He followed briskly through the mizzle the way he had chosen, exalted, fashioning intricate festoons of words. It occurred to him, and he took great pleasure in working out this little figure, that the locus of his fall from the vague grace of the drink had intersected with that of his rise thereunto at its most agreeable point. That was beyond a doubt what had happened. Sometimes the drink-line looped the loop like an eight and if you had got what you were looking for on the way up you got it again on the way down. The bumless eight of the drink-figure. You did not end up where you started, but coming down you met yourself going up. Sometimes, as now, you were glad; more times you were sorry and hastened on to your new home.

Suddenly walking through the rain was not enough, stepping out smartly, buttoned up to the chin, in the cold and the wet, was an inadequate thing to be doing. He stopped on the crown of Baggot Street bridge, took off his reefer, laid it on the parapet and sat down beside it. The Guard was forgotten. Stooping forward then where he sat and flexing his leg until the knee was against his ear and the heel caught on the parapet (admirable posture) he took off his boot and laid it beside the reefer. Then he let down that leg and did the same with the other. Next, resolved to get full value from the bitter nor'-wester that was blowing, he slewed himself right round. His feet dangled over the canal and he saw, lurching across the remote hump of Leeson Street bridge, trams like hiccups-o'-the-wisp. Distant lights on a dirty night, how he loved them, the dirty low-church Protestant! He felt very chilly. He took off his jacket and belt and laid them with the other garments on the parapet. He unbuttoned the top of his filthy old trousers and coaxed out his German shirt. He bundled the skirt of the shirt under the fringe of his pullover and rolled them up clockwise together until they were hooped fast across his thorax. The rain beat against his chest and belly and trickled down. It was even more agreeable than he had anticipated, but very cold. It was now, beating his bosom thus bared to the mean storm vaguely with marble palms, that he took leave of himself and felt wretched and sorry for what he had done. He had done wrong, he realised that, and he was heartily sorry. He sat on, drumming his stockinged heels sadly against the stone, wondering whence on earth could comfort spring, when suddenly the thought of the bottle he had bought pierced his gloomy condition like a beacon. It was there at hand in his pocket, a breast of Bisquit in the pocket of his reefer. He dried himself as best he might with his cambric pochette and adjusted his clothes. When everything was back in place, the reefer buttoned up as before, the boots laced and not a hole skipped, then, but not a moment before, he permitted himself to drink the bottle at a single gulp. The effect of this was to send what is called a glow of warmth what is called coursing through his veins. He squelched off down the street at a trot, resolved to make it, in so far as he had the power to do so, a non-stop run to Casa Frica. Jogging along with his elbows well up he prayed that his appearance might not provoke too much comment.

His mind, in the ups and downs of the past hour, had not had leisure to dwell upon the sufferings in store for it. Even the Alba's scarlet gown – for the qualified assurance of the Venerilla, that it buttoned up with the help of God, had not been of a nature to purge it altogether of misgiving – had ceased to be a burden. But now, when the Frica came pattering out of the mauve salon to intercept him in the vestibule and with her presence shocked him into something worse than sobriety, the full seriousness of his position came home to him with the force of an abstract calamity.

'There you are' she whinnied 'at long last.'

'Here' he said rudely 'I float.'

She recoiled with bursting eyes and clapped a hand to her teeth. Was it possible that he had been courting damp death and damnation or something of the kind? The wet dripped off him as he stood aghast before her and gathered in a little pool at his feet. How dilated her nostrils were!

'You must get out of those wet things' said the Frica, she must hurry now and put the lens in the keyhole, 'this very moment. But the dear boy is drenched to the ... skin!' There was no nonsense about the Frica. When she meant skin she said skin. 'Every stitch' she gloated 'must come off at once, this very instant.'

From the taut cock of the face viewed as a whole, and in particular from the horripilating detail of the upper-lip-writhing up and away in a kind of a duck or a cobra sneer to the quivering snout, he derived the impression that something had inflamed her. And right enough a condition of the highest mettle and fettle had followed hard upon her asinine dumfusion. For here indeed was an unexpected little bit of excitement! In a moment she would break into a caper. Belacqua thought it might be as well to take this disposition in time.

'No' he said composedly, 'if I might have a towel ...'

'A towel!' The scoff was so chocked that she was obliged to blow her nose better late than never.

'It would take off the rough wet' he said.

The rough wet! But how too utterly absurd to speak of the rough wet when it was clear to be seen that he was soaked through and through.

'To the skin!' she cried.

'No' he said, 'if I might just have a towel ...'

Calcken, though deeply chagrined as may well be imagined, knew her man well enough to realise that his determination to accept no more final comfort at her hands than the loan of a towel was unalterable. Also in the salon her absence was beginning to make itself heard, the mice were beginning to enjoy themselves. So off she pattered with a sour look – goose, thought Belacqua, flying barefoot from McCabe – and was back in no time with a hairy towel of great size and a hand-towel.

'You'll get your death' she said, with the adenoidal asperity that he knew so well, and left him. Rejoining her guests she felt that all this had happened to her before, by hearsay or in a dream.

Chas, conversing in low tones with the Shawly, was waiting in some trepidation to be called on for his contribution. This was the famous occasion when Chas, as though he had taken leave of his senses or begun to be irked by his brand-new toga virilis, concluded an unexceptionable recitation with the quatrain:

Toutes êtes, serez ou fûtes,
De fait ou de volonté, putes,
Et qui bien vous chercheroit
Toutes putes vous trouveroit.

The Alba, whom in order to rescue Belacqua we were obliged to abandon just as with characteristic impetuosity she swallowed the pill, opened her campaign by sending Mr Higgins and the P.B. flying, there is no other word for it, about their business. Upon which, not deigning to have any share in the sinister kiss-me-Charley hugger-mugger that had spread like wildfire throughout the building, till it raged from attic to basement, under the aegis of the rising strumpet and the casual cicisbeo, she proceeded in her own quiet and inimitable style to captivate all those who had curbed their instinct to join in the vile necking expressly in order to see what they could make of this pale little person so self-possessed and urbane in the best sense in the scarlet costume. So that, from the point of view of her Maker and in the absence of Belacqua, she was quite a power for good that evening in Casa Frica.

It had not occurred to her, fond as she was of that shabby hero in her own rather stealthy and sinuous fashion, to miss him or think of him at all unless possibly as a rather acute spectator whose eyes behind his glasses upon her and vernier of appraisement going like mad might have slightly spiced her fun. Among the many whom the implacable Frica had hounded from the joys of sense she had marked down for her own one of the grave Jews, him with the bile-tinged conjunctivae, and the merchant prince. She addressed herself to the Jew, but too slackly, as to an insipid dish, and was repulsed. Scarcely had she reloaded and trained her charms more nicely upon this interesting miscreant, of whom she proposed, her mind full of hands rubbing, to make a most salutary example, than the Frica, still smarting under her frustration, announced in a venomous tone of voice that Monsieur Jean du Chas, too well known to the Dublin that mattered for the most talentuous nonesuch that he was to require any introduction, had kindly consented to set the ball a-rolling. Notwithstanding the satisfaction that would have accrued to the Alba had Chas died the death without further delay, she made no attempt to restrain her merriment, in which of course she was uproariously seconded by the P.B., when he came out with the iniquitous apothegm quoted above, and the less so as she observed how bitter-sweetly the paleographer and Parabimbi, who had been surprised by the Frica being slightly naughty together, dissociated themselves from the applause that greeted his descent from the estrade.

This, roughly speaking, was the position when Belacqua framed himself in the doorway.

Surveying him as he stood bedraggled under the lintel, clutching his enormous glasses (a precautionary measure that he never neglected when there was the least danger of his *appearing* embarrassed, appearing in italics because he was always embarrassed), bothered seriously in his mind by a neat little point that had arisen out of nowhere in the vestibule, waiting no doubt for some kind friend to lead him to a seat, the Alba thought she had never seen anybody, man or woman, look quite such a sovereign booby. Seeking to be God, she thought, in the slavish arrogance of a piffling evil.

'Like something' she said to her neighbour the P.B. 'that a dog would bring in.'

The P.B. played up, he overbade.

'Like something' he said 'that, on reflection, he would not.'

He crackled and snuffled over this sottish mot as though it were his own.

In an unsubduable movement of misericord the Alba started out of her chair.

'Nino' she called, without shame or ceremony.

The distant call came to Belacqua like a pint of Perrier to drink in a dungeon. He stumbled towards it.

'Move up in the bed' she ordered the P.B. 'and make room.'

Everybody in the row had to move up one. Like the totem chorus, thought the Alba with complacency, in Rose Marie. Belacqua came down on the end seat thus freed like a sack of potatoes. Observe, now at last they are juxtaposed. His next difficulty was how to get her on his other side, for he could not bear on any account to be on a person's right hand, without finding himself stuck up against the P.B. as a result. Though it scarcely required an expert statistician to realise that the desired order could only be established by his changing places with the P.B., leaving the Alba where she was, yet he wasted much valuable time, in a fever of notes of exclamation, failing to understand that of the six ways in which they could arrange themselves only one satisfied his conditions. He sat not looking, his head sunk, plucking vaguely at his filthy old trousers. When she placed her hand on his sleeve he roused himself and looked at her. To her disgust he was shedding tears.

'At it again' she said.

The Parabimbi could bear it no longer. Clutching and clawing and craning her neck all over the suffocating paleographer she demanded in a general way:

'What's that? Who's that? Is that promessi?'

'I was amazed' said a voice, 'truly amazed, to find Sheffield more hilly than Rome.'

Belacqua made a stupendous effort to acknowledge the cordial greeting of the P.B., but could not. He longed to subside on the floor and pillow his head on the slight madder thigh of his one and only.

'The bicuspid' from the Ovoidologist 'monotheistic fiction ripped by the sophists, Christ and Plato, from the violated matrix of pure reason.'

Who shall silence them, at last? Who shall circumcise their lips from speaking, at last?

The Frica insisted that she trod the estrade.

'Maestro Gormely' she said 'will now play.'

Maestro Gormely executed Scarlatti's Capriccio, without the least aid or accompaniment, on the viol d'amore. This met with no success to speak of.

'Plato!' sneered the P.B. 'Did I hear the word Plato? That dirty little Borstal Boehme!' That was a sockdologer for someone if you like.

'Mr Larry O'Murcahaodha' – the Frica pronounced it as though he were a connection of Hiawatha – 'will now sing.'

Mr Larry O'Murcahaodha tore a greater quantity than seemed fair of his native speech-material to flat tatters.

'I can't bear it' said Belacqua, 'I can't bear it.'

The Frica threw the Poet into the breach. She informed the assistance that it was privileged.

'I think I am accurate in saying' she presented her teeth for the lie 'one of his most recent compositions.'

'Vinegar' moaned Belacqua 'on nitre.'

'Don't you try' said with forced heartiness the Alba, who began to fear for her wretched adorer, 'to put across the Mrs Gummidge before the coverture on me.'

He had no desire, oh none, to put across the Mrs Gummidge at any stage of her experience or anything whatever on her or anyone else. His distress was profound and unaffected. He had abandoned all hope of getting her where he wanted her, he could neither be on her left hand nor at her feet. His only remaining concern, before his soul heaved anchor, was to get some kind of friend to scotch a wolf that he could not hold off by the ears very much longer. He leaned across to the Polar Bear.

'I wonder' he said 'could you possibly—'

'Motus!' screamed the bibliomaniac, from the back row.

The P.B. turned a little yellow, as well he might.

'Let the man say his lines' he hissed 'can't you?'

Belacqua said in a loud despairing voice, falling back into position, a foreign word that he would understand.

'What is it?' whispered the Alba.

Belacqua was green, he did the King of Brobdingnag in a quick dumb crambo.

'Curse you' said the Alba, 'what is it?'

'Let the man say his lines' he mumbled, 'why won't you let the man say his lines?'

An outburst of applause unprecedented in the annals of the mauve salon suggested that he might have done so at last.

'Now' said the Alba.

Belacqua helped himself to a deep breath of the rank ambience and then, with the precipitation of one exhibiting a tongue-teaser, rattled off the borrowed quodlibet as follows:

'When with indifference I remember my past sorrow, my mind has indifference, my memory has sorrow. The mind, upon the indifference which is in it, is indifferent; yet the memory, upon the sorrow which is in it, is not sad.'

'Again' she said, 'slower.'

He was getting on nicely with the repeat when the Alba had a sudden idea and stopped him.

'See me home' she said.

'Have you got it' said Belacqua, 'because I haven't.'

She covered his hand with her hand.

'What I want to know' said the Student.

'Will you?' she said.

'I see' said the Man of Law agreeably to Chas 'by the paper that sailors are painting the Eiffel Tower with no fewer than forty tons of yellow.'

The Frica, returning from having seen off the premises some renegade with a thin tale of a train to catch, made as though to regain the estrade. Her face was suffused with indignation.

'Quick' said Belacqua, 'before it starts.'

The Frica came plunging after them, torrents of speed gushed out of her. Belacqua held the street-door open for the Alba, who seemed half inclined to do the polite, to precede him.

'The lady first' he said.

He insisted on their taking a taxi to her home. They found nothing to say on the way. Je t'adore à l'égal. . . . 'Can you pay this man' he said when they arrived 'because I spent my last on a bottle?'

She took money out of her bag and gave it to him and he paid the man off. They stood on the asphalt in front of the gate, face to face. The rain had almost ceased.

'Well' he said, wondering might he hazard a quick baisemain before he went. He released the gesture but she shrank away and unlatched the gate.

Tire la chevillette, la bobinette cherra.

Pardon these French expressions, but the creature dreams in French.

'Come in' she said, 'there's a fire and a bottle.'

He went in. She would sit in a chair and he would sit on the floor at last and her thigh against his baby anthrax would be better than a foment. For the rest, the bottle, some natural tears and in what hair he had left her high-frequency fingers.

Nisscht möööööglich. . . .

Now it began to rain again upon the earth beneath and greatly incommoded Christmas traffic of every kind by continuing to do so without remission for a matter of thirty-six hours. A divine creature, native of Leipzig, to whom Belacqua, round about the following Epiphany, had occasion to quote the rainfall for December as cooked in the Dublin University Fellows' Garden ejaculated:

'himmisacrakrüzidirkenjesusmariaundjosefundblutigeskreuz!'

Like that, all in one word. The things people come out with sometimes!

But the wind had dropped, as it so often does in Dublin when all the respectable men and women whom it delights to annoy have gone to bed, and the rain fell in a uniform untroubled manner. It fell upon the bay, the littoral, the mountains and the plains, and notably upon the Central Bog it fell with a rather desolate uniformity.

So that when Belacqua that uneasy creature came out of Casa Alba in the small hours of the morning it was a case of darkness visible and no mistake. The street-lamps were all extinguished, as were the moon and stars. He stood out well in the midst of the tramlines, inspected every available inch of the firmament and satisfied his mind that it was quite black. He struck a match and looked at his watch. It had stopped. Patience, a public clock would oblige.

His feet pained him so much that he took off his perfectly good boots and threw them away, with best wishes to some early bird for a Merry Christmas. Then he set off to paddle the whole way home, his toes rejoicing in their freedom. But this small gain in the matter of ease was very quickly more than revoked by such a belly-ache as he had never known. This doubled him up more and more till finally he was creeping along with his poor trunk parallel to the horizon. When he came to the bridge over the canal, not Baggot Street, not Leeson Street, but another nearer the sea, he gave in and disposed himself in the knee-and-elbow position on the pavement. Gradually the pain got better.

What was that? He shook off his glasses and stooped his head to see. That was his hands. Now who would have thought that? He began to try would they work, clenching them and unclenching, keeping them moving for the wonder of his weak eyes. Finally he opened them in unison, finger by finger together, till there they were, wide open, face upward, rancid, an inch from his squint, which however slowly righted itself as he began to lose interest in them as a spectacle. Scarcely had he made to employ them on his face than a voice, slightly more in sorrow than in anger this time, enjoined him to move on, which, the pain being so much better, he was only too happy to do.

LOVE AND LETHE

THE TOUGHS, CONSISTING of Mr and Mrs and their one and only Ruby, lived in a small house in Irishtown. When dinner, which they took in the middle of the day, was ended, Mr Tough went to his room to lie down and Mrs Tough and Ruby to the kitchen for a cup of coffee and a chat. The mother was low-sized, pale and plump, admirably preserved though well past the change. She poured the right amount of water into the saucepan and set it to boil.

'What time is he coming?' she said.

'He said about three' said Ruby.

'With car?' said Mrs Tough.

'He hoped with car' answered Ruby.

Mrs Tough hoped so most devoutly, for she had an idea that she might be invited to join the party. Though she would rather have died than stand in the way of her daughter, yet she saw no reason why, if she kept herself in the dicky, there should be any objection to joining in the fun. She shook the beans in the little mill and ground them violently into powder. Ruby, who was neurasthenic on top of everything else, plugged her ears. Mrs Tough, taking a seat at the deal table against the water would be boiling, looked out of the window at the perfect weather.

'Where are you going?' she said. She had the natural curiosity of a mother in what concerns her child.

'Don't ask me' answered Ruby, who was inclined to resent all these questions.

He to whom they referred, who had hopes of calling at three with a car, was the doomed Belacqua and no other.

The water boiling, Mrs Tough rose and added the coffee, reduced the flame, stirred thoroughly and left to simmer. Though it seems a strange way to prepare coffee, yet it was justified by the event.

'Let me put you up some tea' implored Mrs Tough. She could not bear to be idle.

'Ah no' said Ruby 'no thanks really.'

It struck the half-hour in the hall. It was half-past two, that zero hour, in Irishtown.

'Half-two!' ejaculated Mrs Tough, who had no idea it was so late.

Ruby was glad that it was not earlier. The aroma of coffee pervaded the kitchen. She would have just nice time to dream over her coffee. But she knew that this was quite out of the question with her mother wanting to talk, bursting with questions and suggestions. So when the coffee was dispensed and her mother had settled down for the comfortable chat that went with it she unexpectedly said:

'I think, mother, if you don't mind, I'll take mine with me to the lav, I don't feel very well.'

Mrs Tough was used to the whims of Ruby and took them philosophically usually. But this latest fancy was really a little bit too unheard of. Coffee in the lav! What would father say when he heard? However.

'And the rosiner' said Mrs Tough, 'will you have that in the lav too?'

Reader, a rosiner is a drop of the hard.

Ruby rose and took a gulp of coffee to make room.

'I'll have a gloria' she said.

Reader, a gloria is coffee laced with brandy.

Mrs Tough poured into the proffered cup a smaller portion of brandy than in the ordinary way she would have allowed, and Ruby left the room.

We know something of Belacqua, but Ruby Tough is a stranger to these pages. Anxious that those who read this incredible adventure shall not pooh-pooh it as unintelligible we avail ourselves now of this lull, what time Belacqua is on his way, Mrs Tough broods in the kitchen and Ruby dreams over her gloria, to enlarge a little on the latter lady.

For a long period, on account of the beauty of her person and perhaps also, though in lesser degree, the distinction of her mind, Ruby had been the occasion of much wine-shed; but now, in the thirty third or fourth year of her age, she was so no longer. Those who are in the least curious to know what she looked like at the time in which we have chosen to cull her we venture to refer to the Magdalene[1] in the Perugino Pietà in the National Gallery of Dublin, always bearing in mind that the hair of our heroine is black and not ginger. Further than this hint we need not allow her outside to detain us, seeing that Belacqua was scarcely ever aware of it.

The facts of life had reduced her temper, naturally romantic and idealistic in the highest degree, to an almost atomic despair. Her sentimental experience had indeed been unfortunate. Requiring of love, as a younger and more appetising woman, that it should unite or fix her as firmly and as finally as the sun of a binary in respect of its partner, she had come to avoid it more and more as she found, with increasing disappointment and disgust, its effect at each successive manifestation, for she had been in great demand, to be of quite a different order. The result of this erotic frustration was, firstly, to make her eschew the experience entirely; secondly, to recommend her itch for syzygy to more ideal measures, among which she found music and malt the most efficacious; and finally, to send her cater-wauling to the alcove for whatever shabby joys it could afford. These however, embarras de richesse as long as she remained the scornful maiden, were naturally less at pains to solicit one whose sense of proportion had been acquired to the great detriment of her allurements. The grapes of love, set aside as abject in the days of hot blood, turned sour as soon as she discovered a zest for them. As formerly she had recoiled into herself because she would not, so now she did because she could not, except that in her retreat the hope that used to solace her was dead. She saw her life as a series of staircase jests.

Belacqua, paying pious suit to the hem of her garment and gutting his raptures with great complacency at a safe remove, represented precisely the ineffable long-distance paramour to whom as a home-sick meteorite abounding in IT she had sacrificed her innumerable gallants. And now, the metal of stars smothered in earth,

[1] This figure, owing to the glittering vitrine behind which the canvas cowers, can only be apprehended in sections. Patience, however, and a retentive memory have been known to elicit a total statement approximating to the intention of the painter.

the IT run dry and the gallants departed, he appeared, like the agent of an ironical Fortune, to put her in mind of what she had missed and rowel her sorrow for what she was missing. Yet she tolerated him in the hope that sooner or later, in a fit of ebriety or of common or garden incontinence, he would so far forget himself as to take her in his arms.

Join to all this the fact that she had long been suffering from an incurable disorder and been assured positively by no fewer than fifteen doctors, ten of whom were atheists, acting independently, that she need not look forward to her life being much further prolonged, and we feel confident that even the most captious reader must acknowledge not merely the extreme wretchedness of Ruby's situation, but also the verisimilitude of what we hope to relate in the not too distant future. For we assume the irresponsibility of Belacqua, his faculty for acting with insufficient motivation, to have been so far evinced in previous misadventures as to be no longer a matter for surprise. In respect of this apparent gratuity of conduct he may perhaps with some colour of justice be likened to the laws of nature. A mental home was the place for him.

He cultivated Ruby, for whom at no time did he much care, and made careful love in the terms he thought best calculated to prime her for the part she was to play on his behalf, the gist of which, as he revealed when he deemed her ripe, provided that she should connive at his felo de se, which he much regretted he could not commit on his own bottom. How he had formed this resolution to destroy himself we are quite unable to discover. The simplest course, when the motives of any deed are found subliminal to the point of defying expression, is to call that deed ex nihilo and have done. Which we beg leave to follow in the present instance.

The normal woman of sense asks 'what?' in preference to 'why?' (this is very deep) but poor Ruby had always been deficient in that exquisite quality, so that no sooner had Belacqua opened his project than she applied for his reasons. Now though he had none, as we have seen, that he could offer, yet he had armed himself so well at this point, forewarned by the study he had made of his cats-paw's mind, that he was able to pelt her there and then with the best that diligent enquiry could provide: Greek and Roman reasons, Sturm und Drang reasons, reasons metaphysical, aesthetic, erotic, anterotic and chemical, Empedocles of Agrigentum and John of the Cross reasons, in short all but the true reasons, which did not exist, at least not for the purposes of conversation. Ruby, flattened by this torrent of incentive, was obliged to admit that this was not, as she had inclined to suspect, a greenhorn yielding to the spur of a momentary pique, but an adult desperado of fixed and even noble purpose, and from this concession passed to a state almost of joy. She was done in any case, and here was a chance to end with a fairly beautiful bang. So the thing was arranged, the needful measures taken, the date fixed in the spring of the year and a site near by selected, Venice in October having been rejected as alas impracticable. Now the fateful day had come and Ruby, in the posture of Philosopher Square behind Molly Seagrim's arras, sat winding herself up, while Belacqua, in a swagger sports roadster chartered at untold gold by the hour, trod on the gas for Irishtown.

So fiercely indeed did he do this, though so far from being insured against third-party risks he was not even the holder of a driving-licence, that he scored a wake of objurgation as he sped through the traffic. The better-class pedestrians and cyclists turned and stared after him. 'These stream-lined Juggernauts' they said, shaking their heads, 'are a positive menace.' Civic Guards at various points of the city and suburbs took his number. In Pearse Street he smote off the wheel of a growler as cleanly as Peter Malchus's ear after the agony, but did not stop. Further on, in some lowly street or other, the little children playing beds and ball and other games were scattered like chaff. But before the terrible humped Victoria Bridge, its implacable bisection, in a sudden panic at his own temerity he stopped the car, got out and pushed her across with the help of a bystander. Then he drove quietly on through the afternoon and came in due course without further mishap to the house of his accomplice.

Mrs Tough flung open wide the door. She was all over Belacqua, with his big pallid gob much abused with imagined debauches.

'Ruby' she sang, in a third, like a cuckoo, 'Ru-bee! Ru-bee!'

But would she ever change her tune, that was the question.

Ruby dangled down the stairs, with the marks of her teeth in her nether lip where she could persuade no bee to sting her any more.

'Get on your bonnet and shawl' said Belacqua roughly 'and we'll be going.'

Mrs Tough recoiled aghast. This was the first time she had ever heard such a tone turned on her Ruby. But Ruby got into a coat like a lamb and seemed not to mind. It became only too clear to Mrs Tough that she was not going to be invited.

'May I offer you a little refreshment' she said in an icy voice to Belacqua 'before you go?' She could not bear to be idle.

Ruby thought she had never heard anything quite so absurd. Refreshment before they went! It was if and when they returned that they would be in need of refreshment.

'Really mother' she said, 'can't you see we must be off.'

Belacqua chimed in with a heavy lunch at the Bailey. The truth was not in him.

'Off where?' said Mrs Tough.

'Off' cried Ruby, 'just off.'

What a strange mood she is in to be sure, thought Mrs Tough. However. At least they could not prevent her from going as far as the gate.

'Where did you raise the car?' she said.

If you had seen the car you would agree that this was the most natural question.

Belacqua mentioned a firm of motor engineers.

'Oh indeed' said Mrs Tough.

Mr Tough crept to the window and peeped out from behind the curtain. He had worked himself to the bone for his family and he could only afford a safety-bicycle. A bitter look stole over his cyanosis.

Belacqua got in a gear at last, he had no very clear idea himself which, after much clutch-burning, and they shot forward in Hollywood style. Mrs Tough might have been waving to Lot for all the response she received. Was the cut-out by way of being their spokesman? Ruby's parting gird, 'Expect us when you see us', echoed in her ears. On the stairs she met Mr Tough descending. They passed.

'There is something about that young man' called down Mrs Tough 'that I can't relish.'

'Pup' called up Mr Tough.

They increased the gap between them.

'Ruby is very strange' cried down Mrs Tough.

'Slut' cried up Mr Tough.

Though he might be only able to afford a safety-bicycle he was nevertheless a man of few words. There are better things, he thought, going to the bottle, there are better things in this stenching world than Blue Birds.

The pup and slut drove on and on and there was dead silence between them. Not a syllable did they exchange until the car was safely stowed at the foot of a mountain. But when Ruby saw Belacqua open the dicky and produce a bag she thought well to break a silence that was becoming a little awkward.

'What have you got' she said 'in the maternity-bag?'

'Socrates' replied Belacqua 'the son of his mother, and the hemlocks.'

'No' she said, 'codding aside, what?'

Belacqua let fly a finger for each item.

'The revolver and balls, the veronal, the bottle and glasses, and the notice.'

Ruby could not repress a shiver.

'In the name of God' she said 'what notice?'

'The one that we are fled' replied Belacqua, and not another word would he say though she begged him to tell her. The notice was his own idea and he was proud of it. When the time came she would have to subscribe to it whether she liked it or not. He would keep it as a little surprise for her.

They ascended the mountain in silence. Wisps of snipe and whatever it is of grouse squirted out of the heather on all sides, while the number of hares, brooding in their forms, that they started and sent bounding away, was a credit to the gamekeeper. They plunged on and up through the deep ling and whortleberry. Ruby was sweating. A high mesh wire fence, flung like a shingles round the mountain, obstructed their passage.

'What are all the trusses for?' panted Ruby.

Right along on either hand as far as they could see there were fasces of bracken attached to the wire. Belacqua racked his brains for an explanation. In the end he had to give it up.

'God I don't know at all' he exclaimed.

It certainly was the most astounding thing.

Ladies first. Ruby scaled the fence. Belacqua, holding gallantly

back with the bag in his hand, enjoyed a glimpse of her legs' sin-
cerity. It was the first time he had had occasion to take stock of those
parts of her and certainly he had seen worse. They pushed on and
soon the summit, complete with fairy rath, came into view, howbeit
still at a considerable distance.

Ruby tripped and fell, but on her face. Belacqua's strong arms
were at hand to raise her up.

'Not hurt' he kindly enquired.

'This foul old skirt gets in my way' she said angrily.

'It is an encumbrance' agreed Belacqua, 'off with it.'

This struck Ruby as being such a good suggestion that she acted
upon it without further ado and stood revealed as one of those
ladies who have no use for a petticoat. Belacqua folded the skirt
over his arm, there being no room for it in the bag, and Ruby,
greatly eased, stormed the summit in her knickers.

Belacqua, who was in the lead, halted all of a sudden, clapped his
hands, spun round and told Ruby he had got it. He was keenly
conscious of her standing knee-deep in the ling before him, grateful
for a breather and not bothering to ask what.

'They tie those bundles to the wire' he said 'so that the grouse
will see them.'

Still she did not understand.

'And not fly against the fence and hurt themselves.'

Now she understood. The calm way she took it distressed Belacqua. It was to be hoped that the notice would have better success
than this splendid divulgation. Now the ling was up to her garters,
she seemed to be sinking in the heath as in a quicksand. Could it be
that she was giving at the knees?

'Spirits of this mountain' murmured the heart of Belacqua 'keep
me steadfast.'

Now since parking the car they had not seen a living soul.

The first thing they had to do of course when they got to the top
was admire the view, with special reference to Dun Laoghaire
framed to perfection in the shoulders of Three Rock and Kilma-
shogue, the long arms of the harbour like an entreaty in the blue sea.
Young priests were singing in a wood on the hillside. They heard
them and they saw the smoke of their fire. To the west in the valley
a plantation of larches nearly brought tears to the eyes of Belacqua,

till raising those unruly members to the slopes of Glendoo, mottled like a leopard, that lay beyond, he thought of Synge and recovered his spirits. Wicklow, full of breasts with pimples, he refused to consider. Ruby agreed. The city and the plains to the north meant nothing to either of them in the mood they were in. A human turd lay within the rath.

Like fantoccini controlled by a single wire they flung themselves down on the western slope of heath. From now on till the end there is something very secco and Punch and Judy about their proceedings, Ruby looking more bawdy Magdalene than ever, Belacqua like a super out of the Harlot's Progress. He kept putting off opening the bag.

'I thought of bringing the gramophone' he said 'and Ravel's Pavane. Then—'

'Then you thought again' said Ruby. She had a most irritating habit of interrupting.

'Oh yes' said Belacqua, 'the usual pale cast.'

Notice the literary man.

'S'pity' said Ruby, 'it might have made things easier.'

Happy Infanta! Painted by Velasquez and then no more pensums!

'If you would put back your skirt' said Belacqua violently, 'now that you have done walking, you would make things easier for me.'

How difficult things were becoming, to be sure. The least thing might upset the apple cart at this juncture.

Ruby pricked up her ears. Was this a declaration at last? In case it might be she would not oblige him.

'I prefer it off' she said.

Belacqua, staring fiercely at the larches, sulked for a space.

'Well' he grumbled at last, 'shall we have a little drink to start off?'

Ruby was agreeable. He opened the bag as little as possible, put in his hand, snatched out the bottle, then the glasses and shut it quick.

'Fifteen year old' he said complacently, 'on tick.'

All the money he owed for one thing or another. If he did not pull it off now once and for all he would be broke.

'God' he exclaimed, executing a kind of passionate tick-tack through his pockets, 'I forgot the screw.'

'Pah' said Ruby. 'What odds. Knock its head off, shoot its neck off.'

But the screw turned up as it always does and they had a long drink.

'Length without breath' gasped Belacqua, 'that's the idea, Hiawatha at Dublin bar.'

They had another.

'That makes four doubles' said Ruby 'and they say there's eight in a bottle.'

Belacqua held up the bottle. In that case there was something wrong with her statement.

'Never two without three' he said.

They had another.

'O Death in Life' vociferated Belacqua, 'the days that are no more.'

He fell on the bag and ripped out the notice for her inspection. Painted roughly in white on an old number-plate she beheld:

TEMPORARILY SANE

IK–6996 had been erased to make room for this inscription. It was a palimpsest.

Ruby, pot-valiant, let a loud scoff.

'It won't do' she said, 'it won't do at all.'

It was a disappointment to hear her say this. Poor Belacqua. Sadly he held the plate out at arm's length.

'You don't like it' he said.

'Bad' said Ruby, 'very bad.'

'I don't mean the way it's presented' said Belacqua, 'I mean the idea.'

It was all the same what he meant.

'If I had a paddle' she said 'I'd bury it, idea and all.'

Belacqua laid the offensive object face downward in the heather. Now there was nothing left in the bag but the firearm, the ammunition and the veronal.

The light began to die, there was no time to be lost.

'Will you be shot' said Belacqua 'or poisoned? If the former, have you any preference? The heart? The temple? If the latter' passing over the bag, 'help yourself.'

Ruby passed it back.

'Load' she ordained.

'Chevaliers d'industrie' said Belacqua, inserting the ball, 'nearly all blow their brains out. Kreuger proved the rule.'

'We don't exactly die together darling' drawled Ruby 'or do we?'

'Alas' sighed Belacqua 'what can you expect? But a couple of minutes' with a bounteous brandish of the revolver, 'the time it takes to boil an egg, what is that to eternity?'

'Still' said Ruby 'it would have been rather nice to pass out together.'

'The problem of precedence' said Belacqua, as from a rostrum, 'always arises, even as between the Pope and Napoleon.'

' "The Pope the puke" ' quoted Ruby ' "he bleached her soul . . ." '

'But perhaps you don't know that story' said Belacqua, ignoring the irrelevance.

'I do not' said Ruby 'and I have no wish to.'

'Well' said Belacqua 'in that case I will merely say that they solved it in a strictly spatial manner.'

'Then why not we?' said Ruby.

The gas seems to be escaping somewhere.

'We' said Belacqua 'like twins—'

'Are gone astray' sneered Ruby.

'Are slaves of the sand-glass. There is not room for us to run out arm in arm.'

'As though there were only the one in the world' said Ruby. 'Pah!'

'We happen to pine in the same one' said Belacqua, 'that is the difficulty.'

'Well, it's a minor point' said Ruby 'and by all means ladies first.'

'Please yourself' said Belacqua, 'I'm the better shot.'

But Ruby, instead of expanding her bosom or holding up her head to be blown off, helped herself to a drink. Belacqua fell into a passion.

'Damn it' he cried 'didn't we settle all these things weeks ago? Did we or did we not?'

'A settlement was reached' said Ruby, 'certainly.'

'Then why all this bloody talk?'

Ruby drank her drink.

'And leave us a drop in the bottle' he snarled, 'I'll need it when you're gone.'

That indescribable sensation, compound of exasperation and relief, relaxing, the better to grieve, the coenaesthesis of the consultant when he finds the surgeon out, now burst inside Belacqua. He felt suddenly hot within. The bitch was backing out.

Though whiskey as a rule helped Ruby to feel starry, yet somehow on this occasion it failed to affect her in that way, which is scarcely surprising if we reflect what a very special occasion it was. Now to her amazement the revolver went off, harmlessly luckily, and the bullet fell in terram nobody knows where. But for fully a minute she thought she was shot. An appalling silence, in the core of which their eyes met, succeeded the detonation.

'The finger of God' whispered Belacqua.

Who shall judge of his conduct at this crux? Is it to be condemned as wholly despicable? Is it not possible that he was gallantly trying to spare the young woman embarrassment? Was it tact or concupiscence or the white feather or an accident or what? We state the facts. We do not presume to determine their significance.

'Digitus Dei' he said 'for once.'

The remark rather gives him away, does it not?

When the first shock of surprise had passed and the silence spent its fury a great turmoil of life-blood sprang up in the breasts of our two young felons, so that they came together in inevitable nuptial. With the utmost reverence at our command, moving away on tiptoe from where they lie in the ling, we mention this in a low voice.

It will quite possibly be his boast in years to come, when Ruby is dead and he an old optimist, that at least on this occasion, if never before nor since, he achieved what he set out to do; car, in the words of one competent to sing of the matter, l'Amour et la Mort — caesura — n'est qu'une mesme chose.

May their night be full of music at all events.

WALKING OUT

ONE FATEFUL FINE Spring evening he paused, not so much in order to rest as to have the scene soak through him, out in the middle of the late Boss Croker's Gallops, where no horses were to be seen any more. Pretty Polly that great-hearted mare was buried in the vicinity. To stroll over this expanse in fine weather, these acres of bright green grass, was almost as good as to cross the race-course of Chantilly with one's face towards the Castle. Leaning now on his stick, between Leopardstown down the hill to the north and the heights of Two Rock and Three Rock to the south, Belacqua regretted the horses of the good old days, for they would have given to the landscape something that the legions of sheep and lambs could not give. These latter were springing into the world every minute, the grass was spangled with scarlet after-births, the larks were singing, the hedges were breaking, the sun was shining, the sky was Mary's cloak, the daisies were there, everything was in order. Only the cuckoo was wanting. It was one of those Spring evenings when it is a matter of some difficulty to keep God out of one's meditations.

Belacqua leaned all his spare weight on the stick and took in the scene, in a sightless passionate kind of way, and his Kerry Blue bitch sat on the emerald floor beside him. She was getting old now, she could not be bothered hunting any more. She could tree a cat, that was no bother, but beyond that she did not care to go. So she just remained seated, knowing perfectly well that there were no cats in Croker's Gallops, and did not care very much what happened. The bleating of the lambs excited her slightly.

My God, it occurred to Belacqua, I must be past my best when I find myself preferring this time of year to the late Autumn.

This vivid thought, quite irrefutable as he recognised at once, did not so distress him that he was unable to move on. Past the worst of his best, there was nothing so very terrible in that, on the contrary. Soon he might hope to be creeping about in a rock-garden with tears in his eyes. Indeed proof, if proof be needed, that he was rather elated than distressed, appears in his taking his weight off the stick and moving forward; for the effect of a real dereliction was always to cast him up high and dry and unable to stir. The bitch walked behind. She was hot and bored.

Slowly he raised his eyes till they were levelled at his destination. Tom Wood, it graced like a comb a low hill in the distance. There he had assignation, but only in the sense that an angler has with the fish in a river. He had been there so often that he knew all its ins and outs, yet he could not have given a name to its timber. Oak, he supposed vaguely, or elm, but even had he looked he would not have been any wiser. This country lad, he could not tell an oak from an elm. Larches however he knew, from having climbed them as a little fat boy, and a young plantation of these, of a very poignant reseda, caught his eye now on the hillside. Poignant and assuasive at once, the effect it had upon him as he advanced was prodigious.

He thought if only his wife would consent to take a cicisbeo how pleasant everything would be all round. She knew how he loved her and yet she would not hear of his getting her a cicisbeo. He was merely betrothed, but already he thought of his fiancée as his wife, an anticipation that young men undertaking this change of condition might be well advised to imitate. Time and again he had urged her to establish their married life on this solid basis of a cuckoldry. She understood and appreciated his sentiment, she acknowledged that his argument was sound, and yet she would not or could not bring herself to act accordingly. He was not a bad-looking young fellow, a kind of cretinous Tom Jones. She would kill his affection with her nonsense before the wedding bells, that would be the end of it.

Turning this and cognate anxieties over and over in his mind he came at length to the southern limit of the Gallops and the by-road that he had to cross to get into the next list of fields. Thus, large tracts of champaign, hedges and ditches and blessed grass and daisies, then the deep weal of road, again and again, until he would come to the wood. The wall was too high for the bitch at her time of life, so he helped her across with a vigorous heave on the grey hunkers. This gave him pleasure if he had stopped to analyse it. But himself, he made short work of the obstacle, thinking: what a splendid thing it is when all is said and done to be young and vigorous.

In the ditch on the far side of the road a strange equipage was installed: an old high-wheeled cart, hung with rags. Belacqua looked round for something in the nature of a team, the crazy yoke could scarcely have fallen from the sky, but nothing in the least resembling a draught-beast was to be seen, not even a cow. Squatting under the cart a complete down-and-out was very busy with something or other. The sun beamed down on this as though it were a new-born lamb. Belacqua took in the whole outfit at a glance and felt, the wretched bourgeois, a paroxysm of shame for his capon belly. The bitch, in a very remote manner, stepped up to the cart and sniffed at the rags.

'Cmowathat!' vociferated the vagabond.

Now Belacqua could see what he was doing. He was mending a pot or a pan. He beat his tool against the vessel in his anxiety. But the bitch made herself at home.

'Wettin me throusers' said the vagabond mildly 'wuss 'n meself.'

So that was his trousers!

This privacy which he had always assumed to be inalienable, this ultimate prerogative of the Christian man, had now been violated by somebody's pet. Yet he might have been calling a score, his voice was so devoid of rancour. But Belacqua was embarrassed in the last degree.

'Good evening' he piped in fear and trembling 'lovely evening.'

A smile proof against all adversity transformed the sad face of the man under the cart. He was most handsome with his thick, if unkempt, black hair and moustache.

'Game ball' he said.

After that further comment was impossible. The question of apology or compensation simply did not arise. The instinctive nobility of this splendid creature for whom private life, his joys and chagrins at evening under the cart, was not acquired, as Belacqua one day if he were lucky might acquire his, but antecedent, disarmed all the pot-hooks and hangers of civility. Belacqua made an inarticulate flourish with his stick and passed down the road out of the life of this tinker, this real man at last.

But he had not gone far, he had not yet turned aside into the next zone of field, before he heard cries behind him and the taratantara of hooves. This was none other than his dearest Lucy, his betrothed, astride her magnificent jennet. Reining in she splashed past him in a positive tornado of caracoling. When her mount had calmed down and her own panting somewhat abated she explained to the astonished and, be it said, somewhat vexed Belacqua how she came to be there.

'Oh, I called round and they told me you were gone out.'

Belacqua caressed the soft jowl of the jennet. Poor beast, it had been ridden into a lather. It looked at him with a very white eye. It would tolerate his familiarities since of such was its servitude, but it hoped, before it died, to bite a man.

'So I didn't know what to do, so what do you think?'

Belacqua could not imagine. There seemed to be nothing to do under the circumstances but make the best of it.

'I got up on the roof and did the Sister Ann.'

'No!' exclaimed Belacqua. This was pleasant.

'Yes, and I found you in the end, all alone in the Gallops.'

This was charming. Belacqua came over to her leg.

'Darling!' she ejaculated.

'Well' he said 'well well well.'

'So I skirted round by the road' she was overcome by the success of her little manoeuvre 'and here I am.'

She had rounded him up, she had cut him off, it was nearly as good as catching an ocean greyhound on the pictures. He kissed her flexed knee.

'Brava!'

To think that somebody needed him in this way! He could not but be touched.

In face and figure Lucy was entrancing, her entire person was quite perfect. For example, she was as dark as jet and of a paleness that never altered, and her thick short hair went back like a pennon from her fanlight forehead. But it would be waste of time to itemise her. Truly there was no fault or flaw in the young woman. Yet we feel we must say before we let her be, her poor body that must wither, that her nether limbs, from where they began even unto where they ended, would have done credit to a Signorelli page. Let us put it this way, that through her riding-breeches they came through. What more can be said for a woman's legs, thighs included? Or is all this merely ridiculous?

Belacqua wondered, when the first rapture at having been spied from afar had worn off, what the hell she wanted. But it appeared that she did not want anything in particular, she just wanted to be with him. This was a falsehood of course, she did want something in particular. However.

'Listen my dear Lucy' he said with a kind of final franchise 'I know you won't mind if I can't spend this evening with my' – it took him some time to find a term of endearment to cover the facts – 'my Fünklein.'

But she pulled a very bitter face. This lizard of hers, he seemed to be making a habit of giving her the go-by, very soon if he did not watch out she would have no use for him.

'I have the chinks' he complained and apologised. 'God help me, I'm no fit company for anyone let alone lovely Lucy.'

Indeed she was better than lovely, with its suggestion of the Nobel Yeats, with her jet of hair and her pale set face, the whipcord knee and the hard bust sweating a little inside the black jersey.

Now it is her turn to go on.

Does he really imagine, she wondered, that it is his company I want, which seems to me at this stage about as futile an article as a pen-wiper. Let the ink clot on the nib, let the wine, to put it another way, scour the lees.

He spoke, as she knew he was bound to, if only she held her pose long enough.

'I went out to walk it off.'

'Walk what off?' cried Lucy. She was sick and tired of his moods.

'Oh I don't know' he said, 'our old friend, the devil's bath.'

He drew designs with his devil's finger on the jennet's coat, wondering how to put it.

'Then I thought' he said at last 'that the best thing to do was to go to the wood for a little sursum corda.'

This was another falsehood, because the wood had been in his thoughts all day. He told it with a kind of miserable conviction.

'Corda is good' said Lucy.

As she uttered these words with one of her smart smiles the

truth, or something that seemed very like it, struck her with such violence that she nearly fell out of the saddle. But she recovered herself and Belacqua, back at the bridle courting disaster, saw nothing.

'I know' he said sadly 'you don't believe in these private experiences, women don't I know as a rule. And if you distrust them now—'

He stopped, and it was obvious, even to the jennet, that he had gone too far.

What was the bitch doing all this time? She was sitting in the ditch, listening.

The sun seemed to be sinking in the south, for the group was now wholly in the shadow of the high hedge on Lucy's left, though to be sure on her right the Gallops were still shining. Though the larks had gone to bed and the rooks were going there was no loss of pastoral clamour, for the lambs cried more loudly as the light fell and dogs began to bark in the distance. The cuckoo however was still in abeyance. Belacqua stepped back into the ditch and stood irresolute beside his pet, the jennet drooped its head and closed its eyes, Lucy sat very still on its back staring straight before her, they all seemed to be listening, the woman, the bitch, the jennet and the man. The vagabond could see them between adjoining spokes of his wheel, by moving his head into the right position he was far enough away to frame the whole group in a sector of his wheel.

Lucy, resolved to put her terrible surmise to the proof, had very soon shamed her lover into making terms, for of course he was as wax in her hands[1] when it came to a course of action. It was arranged that they should meet at the gate that led off the lane into the wood, he going his way across country direct and she, because it was out of the question to negotiate walls and dikes with the jennet, her devious one by road. What adverse fate forbade them at this point to fund their ways? The group broke up and soon the vagabond, peering out through his sector, saw only the grey of the road with its green hem.

Lucy jogged along briskly. We may mention that the effect of this motion was usually to exhilarate her, but it did not do so now, so stunned was she by the sudden vision of Belacqua that damned him,

[1] Cp. Fingal.

were it true, as her mate, her partner in life's journey. If what she dreaded were true her heart was broken, to say nothing of her engagement. But could it? This young man of good family, so honourable to her certain knowledge in all his dealings, so spiritual, a Varsity man too, could he be such a creepy-crawly? It seemed inconceivable that she should have been so blinded to his real nature as to let her love, born in a spasm more than a year ago in the Portrush Palais de Danse, increase steadily from day to day till now it amounted to something like a morbid passion. Yet at the same time she was forced to admit how perfectly the horrible diagnosis which had just been revealed to her fitted in with certain aspects of his behaviour that she had never been able to fathom: all his baby talk, for example, of her living with him like a music while being the wife in body of another; all his fugues into 'sursum corda' and 'private experience', from the inception of their romance, when he used to leave her in the evening and prowl among the sandhills, until now, the very eve of their nuptials, a time that she would always think of, whatever its upshot, as throttled in a pinetum.

There even now a pretty little German girl subsided, with a 'wie heimlich!' on the bed of needles alongside her Harold's Cross Tanzherr.

The way screwed uphill between the hedges of red may. Lucy, anxious to be the first to arrive, kept the jennet at the trot, digging in her knees and timing the rise and fall of the difficult motion to a nicety. Yet her engrossment was so profound that she might have had privet on either hand for all she knew or cared, so that the blossom, fading now in a most beautiful effect as the shadows lengthened, was quite lost on the unhappy horsewoman. She saw nothing of the wood, the root of all the mischief, that loomed directly at some little distance before her, its outposts of timber serried enough to make a palisade, but not so closely as to screen the secret things beyond them. She was spared the high plume of smoke waxing and waning, like a Lied, fume of signs, against the dark green of the pines.

Belacqua saw these things, the trees, the plume of smoke, the may, dead lambs also lying in the hedgetops, all the emblems of the spring of the year. He would. And Lucy, groping in a sudden chaos of mind, saw nothing. Poor little Lucy! The more she struggled to eject the idea that possessed her ever since those careless words: 'Corda is good', the more it seemed to prevail to the exclusion of all others. The derogation of her gentle Belacqua from one whom she had loved in all the shadow and tangles of his conduct to a trite spy of the vilest description was not to be set aside by a girl of her mettle merely on account of its being a great shock to her sentimental system. The two Belacquas, the old and dear enigma and now this patent cad, played cruel battledore with her mind. But she would decide between them before she slept, how she did not know, she had laid no plan, but somehow she would do it. Whatever loathing the truth might beget within her, was it not better to be sure than sorry?

Now it was definitely dusk.

A superb silent limousine, a Daimler no doubt, driven by a drunken lord, swept without warning round a bend in the narrow round and struck the jennet a fearful blow in the sternum. Lucy came a sickening cropper backwards down the rampant hindquarters, the base of her spine, then of her skull, hit the ground a double welt, the jennet fell on top of her, the wheels of the car jolted over what was left of the jennet, who expired there and then in the twilight, sans jeter un cri. Lucy however was not so fortunate, being crippled for life and her beauty dreadfully marred.

Now it is Belacqua's turn to carry on.

He arrived in due course at the rendezvous, expecting to find Lucy there before him, for he had loitered on the way to marvel at the evening effects. He climbed the gate and sat down on the grass to await her arrival, but of course she did not turn up.

'Damn it' he said at last to the bitch 'does she expect me to wait here all night?'

He gave her five more minutes, then he rose and walked up the hill till he came to the skirts of the wood. There he turned and combed the darkling landscape with his weak eyes. Just as she but a short time back had stood on the housetop and looked for him eagerly and found him, so he did now standing on the hilltop in respect of her, with this difference however, that his eagerness was so slight that he was rather relieved than otherwise when he could see no sign of her. Gradually indeed he ceased to look for her and looked at the scene instead.

It was at this moment that he heard with a pang, rattling away in the distance, crex-crex, crex-crex, crex-crex, the first corncrake of the season. With a pang, because he had not yet heard the cuckoo. He could not help feeling that there must be something wrong somewhere when a man who had been listening day after day for the cuckoo suddenly heard the corncrake instead. The velvet third of the former bird, with its promise of happiness, was denied him, and the death-rattle of one that he had never seen proposed in its place. It was a good thing for Belacqua that he set no store by omens. He tethered the bitch to a tree, switched on his pineal eye and entered the wood.

With all the delays that he had been put to on Lucy's account he was long past his usual time and it was very dark in the wood. He drew blank in all the usual coverts and was just about to give it up as a bad job and wend his way home when he suddenly spied a flutter and a gleam of white in a hollow. This was Fräulein and friend. Belacqua came up on them cautiously from behind and watched for a short time. But for once, whatever was the matter with him, he seemed to find but little zest in the performance, so little indeed that he surprised himself not looking at all but staring vacantly into the shadows, alive to nothing but the weight and darkness and silence of the wood bearing down on top of him. It was all very submarine and oppressive.

He roused himself finally and moved away on tiptoe over the moss that would not betray him. He would go home and sit with Lucy and play the gramophone and see how he felt then. But he stumbled against a rotten bough growing close to the ground, it snapped off with a loud report and he fell forward on his face. Then, almost before he knew what had happened, he was running in and out through the trees with the infuriated Tanzherr pounding along behind in hot pursuit.

Any advantage that familiarity with the ground may have conferred on Belacqua was liberally outweighed by the condition of his feet that were so raw with one thing and another that even to walk was painful, while to run was torture. As he neared the point where he had tethered the bitch and entered the wood he realised that he was being overhauled fast and that there was nothing for it but to turn and give battle. Shortening his grasp of the stick and slackening his pace as he ran clear of the trees he stopped abruptly, turned and with both hands thrust the sharp ferrule at the hypogastrium of his pursuer. This blow, however well conceived, was prematurely delivered. The Tanzherr saw it on its way, jazzed neatly out of the line, skidded round, lowered his head, charged, crashed into his quarry and bore him to the ground.

Now a fierce struggle ensued. Belacqua, fighting like a woman, kicking, clawing, tearing and biting, put up a gallant resistance. But his strength was as little as his speed and he was soon obliged to cry mercy. Whereupon the victor, holding him cruelly by the nape face downward, adminstered a brutal verberation with the stick. The bitch, to do her justice, strained at her tether. The Fräulein, wraith-like in the gloom in her flimsy white frock, came to the edge of the wood and watched, rapt, clutching her bosom, valour towards men being an emblem of ability towards women.

Belacqua's screams grew fainter and fainter and at length the Tanzherr, his fury appeased, desisted, launched a parting kick and swaggered off with his girly under his brawny arm.

How long he lay there, half insensible, he never knew. It was black night when he crept painfully to the bitch and released her. Nor has he ever been able to understand how he reached home, crawling rather than climbing over the various hedges and ditches, leaving the bitch to follow as best she could. So much for his youth and vigour.

But tempus edax, for now he is happily married to Lucy and the question of cicisbei does not arise. They sit up to all hours playing the gramophone, An die Musik is a great favourite with them both, he finds in her big eyes better worlds than this, they never allude to the old days when she had hopes of a place in the sun.

WHAT A
MISFORTUNE

BELACQUA WAS SO happy married to the crippled Lucy that he tended to be sorry for himself when she died, which she did on the eve of the second anniversary of her terrible accident,[1] after two years of great physical suffering borne with such fortitude as only women seem able to command, having passed from the cruellest extremes of hope and despair that ever sundered human heart to their merciful resolution, some months before her decease, in a tranquillity of acquiescence that was the admiration of her friends and no small comfort to Belacqua himself.

Her death came therefore as a timely release and the widower, to the unutterable disgust of the deceased's acquaintance, wore none of the proper appearances of grief. He could produce no tears on his own account, having as a young man exhausted that source of solace through over-indulgence; nor was he sensible of the least need or inclination to do so on hers, his small stock of pity being devoted entirely to the living, by which is not meant this or that particular unfortunate, but the nameless multitude of the current quick, life, we dare almost say, in the abstract. This impersonal pity was damned in many quarters as an intolerable supererogation and in some few as a positive sin against God and Society. But Belacqua could not help it, for he was alive to no other kind than this: final, uniform and continuous, unaffected by circumstance, assigned without discrimination to all the undead, without works. The public, taking cognisance of it only as callousness in respect of this or that wretched individual, had no use for it; but its private advantages were obviously very great.

All the hags and faggots, male and female, that he had ever seen or heard of, inarticulate with the delicious mucus of sympathy, disposed in due course of that secretion, when its flavour had been

[1] Cp. Walking Out.

quite exhausted, viva sputa and by letter post, through the emunctory of his bereavement. He felt as though he had been sprayed from head to foot with human civet and would never again be clean or smell sweet, i.e. of himself, whose odours he snuffed up at all times with particular complacency. These however began to reassert themselves as time ran out and the spittle of the hags, while Lucy's grave subsided, grew green and even began to promise daisies, was introverted upon their own sores and those more recent of their nearest and dearest. Restored to these dearworthy effluvia, lapped in this pungent cocoon as the froghopper in its foam, Belacqua would walk in his garden and play with the snapdragons. To kneel before them in the dust and the clay of the ground and throttle them gently till their tongues protruded, at that indigo hour when the only barking (to consider but a single pastoral motiv) to be heard was that which could be scarcely heard, released so far away under the mountains that it came as a pang of sound of just the right severity, was the recreation he found best suited to his melancholy at this season and most satisfying to that fairy tale need of his nature whose crises seemed to correspond with those of his precious ipsissimosity, if such a beautiful word may be said to exist. It pleased his fancy to think of himself as a kind of easy-going Saint George at the Court of Mildendo.

The snapdragons were beginning to die of their own accord and Belacqua to feel more and more the lack of those windows on to better worlds that Lucy's big black eyes had been, when he woke up one fine afternoon to find himself madly in love with a girl of substance – a divine frenzy, you understand, none of your lewd passions. This lady he served at his earliest convenience with a tender of his hand and fortune which, however inconsiderable, had a certain air of distinction, being unearned. First she said no, then oh no, then oh really, then but really, then, in ringing tones, yes sweetheart.

When we say a girl of substance we mean that her promissory wad, to judge by her father's bearing in general and in particular by his respiration after song, was, so to speak, short-dated. To deny that Belacqua was alive to this circumstance would be to present him as an even greater imbecile than he was when it came to seeing the obvious; whereas to suggest that it was implied, however slightly, in his brusque obsession with the beneficiary to be, would constitute such obloquy as we do not much care to deal in. Let us therefore put forth a minimum of charity and observe in a casual way, with eyes cast down and head averted until the phrase has ceased to vibrate, that he happened to conceive one of his Olympian fancies for a fairly young person with expectations. We can't straddle the fence nicer than that.

Her name it was Thema bboggs, younger daughter of Mr and Mrs Otto Olaf bboggs. She was not beautiful in the sense that Lucy was; nor could she be said to transcend beauty, as the Alba seemed to do, nor yet to have slammed her life and person in its face, as Ruby perhaps had. She brought neither the old men running nor the young men to a standstill. To be quite plain she was and always had been so definitely not beautiful that once she was seen she was with difficulty forgotten, which is more than can be said for, say, the Venus Callipyge. Her trouble was to get herself seen in the first instance. But what she did have, as Belacqua never wearied of asserting to himself, was a most cherharming personality, together with intense appeal, as he repudiated with no less insistence, from the strictly sexual standpoint.

Otto Olaf had made his money in toilet requisites and necessaries. His hobby, since retiring from active participation in the affairs of the splendid firm that was his life-work, brain-child, labour of love and the rest, was choice furniture. He was said to have the finest and most comprehensive collection of choice furniture in North Great George's Street, from which lousy locality, notwithstanding the prayers of his wife and first-born for a home of their own very own in Foxrock, he refused coarsely to remove. The fondest memories of his boyhood, beguiled as a plumber's improver, the most copious sweats and triumphs of his prime, both in business and (with a surly look at Mrs bboggs) the office and affairs of love, from the vernal equinox, in his self-made sanitary phrase, to the summer solstice of his life; all the ups and downs of a strenuous career, instituted in the meanest household fixture and closing now in the glories of Hepplewhites and bombé commodes, were bound up in good old grand old North Great George's Street, in consideration of which he had pleasure in referring his wife and first-born to that portion of himself which he never desired any person to kick nor volunteered to kiss in another.

The one ground lay under Mr bboggs's contempt for Belacqua and
Thelma's consent to be his bride: he was a poet. A poet is indeed a
very nubile creature, dowered, don't you know, with the love of
love, like La Rochefoucauld's woman from her second passion on.
So nubile that the women, God bless them, can't resist them, God
help them. Except of course those intended merely for breeding and
innocent of soul, who prefer, as less likely to upset them, the more
balanced and punctual raptures of a chartered accountant or a pub-
lisher's reader. Now Thelma, however much she left to be desired,
was not a brood-maiden. She had at least the anagram of a good
face, while as for soul, sparkling or still as preferred, it was her
speciality. Which explains how Belacqua had merely to hold out
against no and its derivatives to have her fly in the end, as a swal-
low to its eave or a long losing jenny down the whirlpool of a
pocket, into his keycold embrace.

Mr bboggs, on the other hand, was of Coleridge's opinion that
every literary man ought to have an illiterate profession. Indeed he
seemed to go a step further than Coleridge when he asserted, to the
embarrassment of Mrs bboggs and Thelma, the satisfaction of his
elder daughter Una, for whom an ape had already been set aside in
hell, and the alarm of Belacqua, that when he looked round and saw
what they called a poet allowing his bilge to interfere with his business he developed a Beltschmerz of such intensity that he was
obliged to leave the room. The poet present, observing that Mr
bboggs remained seated, plucked up courage to exclaim:

'Beltschmerz, Mr bboggs sir, did I hear you say?'

Mr bboggs threw back his head until it seemed as though his
dewlap must burst and sang, in the slight sweet tenor that never
failed to electrify those that heard it for the first time:

> 'He wore a belt
> Whenever he felt
> A pain in his tiddlypush,
> A chemical vest
> To cover his chest
> When cannoning off the cush.'

Belacqua said in a grieved tone to Mrs bboggs, appreciation being
most penetrating when oblique:

'I never knew Mr bboggs had such a voice.'

This endowment Mr bboggs, when the dewlap, like a bagful of ferrets, had settled down after a brief convulsion, proceeded to demean further:

'He took quinine . . .'

'Otto' cried Mrs bboggs. 'Enough.'

'As clear as a bell' said Belacqua 'and I was never told.'

'Yes' said Mr bboggs, 'a real quality voice.' He closed his eyes and was back in the bathrooms of his beginnings. 'A trifle fine' he conceded.

'Fine how are you!' cried Belacqua. 'A real three dimensional organ, Mr bboggs sir, I give you my word and honour.'

Mrs bboggs had a lover in the Land Commission, so much so in fact that certain ill-intentioned ladies of her acquaintance lost no occasion to insist on the remarkable disparity, in respect not only of physique but of temperament between Mr bboggs and Thelma: he so sanguine, so blond and solid in every way, which properties, observe, were no less truly to be predicated of his Una; and she such a black wisp of a creature. A most extraordinary anomaly, to put it mildly, and one that could scarcely be ignored by any friend of the family.

The presumptive cuckoo, if not exactly one of those dapper little bureaucrats that give the impression of having come into the world dressed by Austin Reed, presented some of the better-known differentiae: the dimpled chin, the bright brown doggy eyes that were so appealing, the unrippled surface of vast white brow whose area was at least double that of the nether face, and anchored there for all eternity the sodden cowlick that looked as though it were secreting macassar to discharge into his eye. With his high heels he attained to five foot five, his nose was long and straight and his shoes a size and a half too large to bear it out. A plug of moustache cowered at his nostrils like a frightened animal before its lair. At the least sign of danger it would scurry up into an antrum. He expelled his words with gentle discrimination, as a pastry-cook squirts icing upon a cake. He had a dirty mind, great assurance and ability towards women, and a cap for every joke, ancient and modern. He drank just a little in public for the sake of sociability, but made up for it in private. His name was Walter Draffin.

The horns of Otto Olaf sat easily upon him. He knew all there was to be known about Walter Draffin and treated him with special consideration. Any man who saved him trouble, as Walter had for so many years, could rely on his esteem. Thus the treacherous bureaucrat was made free of the house in North Great George's Street where, as formerly he had abused that privilege in the bed of his host, so now he did out of his decanter. Indeed he was subject to such vertiginous satisfactions in his elevated position on Saint Augustine's ladder, the deeds of shame with Mrs bboggs beyond recall in the abyss, that the power to tell himself when would desert him completely.

Bridie bboggs was nothing at all, neither as wife, as Otto Olaf had been careful to ascertain before he made her one, nor as mistress, which suited Walter's taste for moderation in all things. Unless some small positive value be allowed her in right of the fascination which she seemed to exert over her domestic staff, whose obstinacy in the employment of a mistress neutral to the point of idiocy moved such others as were better equipped and worse served to expressions of admiration that were not free of malice, no doubt.

The elder daughter was very dull. Think of holy Juliana of Norwich, to her aspect add a dash of souring, to her tissue half a hundredweight of adipose, abstract the charity and prayers, spray in vain with opopanax and assafoetida, and behold a radiant Una after a Hammam and a face massage. But withal she rejoiced in one accomplishment for which Belacqua had no words to express his respect, namely, an ability to play from memory, given the opening bar, any Mozart sonata whatsoever, with a xylophonic precision and an even-handed mezzo-forte that scorned to observe the least distinction between those notes that were significant and those that were not. Belacqua, anxious to improve his position with Una, who held him and all that pertained to him in the greatest abhorrence, would control these feats, choking with admiration, in Augener's edition: which trouble, however, he very soon learned to spare himself.

A little bird whispered when to Walter Draffin who, with his right hand thus released, drew from his pocket a card and read, printed in silver on an azure ground:

Mr and Mrs Otto Olaf bboggs
request the pleasure of
Mr Walter Draffin's
Company
at the marriage of their daughter
THELMA
with
MR BELACQUA SHUAH
at the Church of Saint Tamar
Glasnevin
on Saturday, 1st August,
at 2.30 P.M.
and afterwards
at 55 North Great George's Street

55 North Great George's Street   R.S.V.P.

How like an epitaph it read, with the terrible sigh in the end-pause of each line. And yet, thought Walter, quenching the conceit as he did so, one might have expected a little enjambment in an invitation to such an occasion. Ha! He drew back his head from the card in order that he might see it as a whole. A typical Bridie bboggs production. What did it remind him of? A Church of Ireland Sunday School certificate of good conduct and regular attendance? No. They had his in the old home locked up in the family Bible, marking the place where Lamentations ended and Ezekiel began. Then perhaps the menu of an Old Boys Reunion Dinner, incorporating the School colours? No. Walter heaved a heavy sigh. He knew it reminded him of something, but what that something was, over and above Bridie and her sense of style, he could not discover. No doubt it would come back to him when he was least expecting it. But his little enjambment joke was pretty hot. He slaked it a second time. The only thing he did not like about it was its slight recondity, so few people knowing what an enjambment was. For example, it could not be expected to convulse a snug. Well, he must just put it into his book.

Under separate cover by the same post he received a note from Mrs bboggs: 'Dear Walter, Both Otto and I are most anxious that you, as such an old friend of the family, should propose the health of the happy couple. We do hope, dear Walter, and I feel confident, that you will.' To which he hastened to reply: 'Dear Bridie, Of course I shall be most happy and honoured to perform.'

Dear Otto Olaf! Wrapped in his tables and chairs and allowing himself to be duped, as he knew, by Walter and, as he thought, by Belacqua. Let Mr Draffin, who had been of service, drink his whiskey, and Thelma, that by-product of a love-encounter, bestow herself on whom she pleased. Let there be a circus wedding by all means, his house invaded and his furniture wrecked. The days that came after would be of better rest. Dear Otto Olaf!

Belacqua prepared to negotiate a loan sufficient to meet his obligations, which fell heavily on a man of his modest condition. There was the ring (Lucy's redeemed), the endless fees relative to the ceremony, duties to vicar, verger, organist, officiating clergymen and bell-ringers, the big bridal bouquet, the little nosegays for the maids, new linen and other indispensable household effects, to say nothing at all of the price of a quick honeymoon, which fiasco, touring Connemara in a borrowed car, he had no intention of allowing to run away with more than a week or ten days.

His best man helped him to work it out over a bottle.

'I do not propose—' said Belacqua, when the average of their independent estimates had been augmented by ten pounds for overhead expenses.

'Overhead!' cackled the best man. 'Very good!'

Belacqua shrank in a most terrifying manner.

'Either I misunderstand you' he said 'or you forget yourself.'

'Beg pardon' said the best man, 'beg pardon, beg pardon. No offence.'

Belacqua came back into the picture at his own convenience.

'I do not propose' he resumed 'to affront you with a gift on this delicate occasion.'

The best man bridled and squirmed at the mere suggestion.

'But' Belacqua made haste to extenuate this refinement of feeling 'if you would care to have the original manuscript of my Hypothalamion, corrected, autographed, dated, inscribed and half-bound in time-coloured skivers, you are more than welcome.'

Capper Quin, for so we must call him, known to his admirers as Hairy, he was so glabrous, and to the ladies as Tiny, he was so enormous, was not merely a bachelor, and thus qualified to attend Belacqua without violence to etiquette, but also one of the coming writers, which accounts for his alacrity to hold the hat of a member of the Cuttings Association. He now choked with gratification.

'Oh' he gasped 'really I ... really you ...' and broke down. To construct a sentence with subject, predicate and object Hairy required a pencil and a sheet of paper.

'Capper' said Belacqua, 'say no more. I'll have it made up for you.'

When Hairy had quite done panting his pleasure he held up his hand.

'Well' said Belacqua.

'Thyme-coloured' said Hairy, and broke down.

'Well' said Belacqua.

'Sage-green' said Hairy. 'Am I right?'

In the dead silence that followed this suggestion Hairy received the impression that his patron's spirit had left its prison, on ticket of leave at all events, and was already casting about for something light and hey nonny that would serve to cover his own departure when Belacqua made answer, in a voice blistered with emotion:

> 'Ouayseau bleheu, couleurre du temps,
> Vole a mouay, promptement.'

and burst into tears.

Hairy rose and trode with penetrating softness to the door. Tact, he thought, tact, tact, the need for tact at a time like this.

'Study our duties' sobbed Belacqua 'and call me not later than twelve.'

The bboggses were gathered together in conclave.

'Thelma' said Una with asperity 'let us kindly have your attention.'

For Thelma's thoughts, truant to the complicated manoeuvres required of a snow-white bride, had flown on the usual wings to Galway, Gate of Connaught and dream of stone, and more precisely to the Church of Saint Nicolas whither Belacqua projected, if it were not closed when they arrived, to repair without delay and kneel, with her on his right hand at last for a pleasant change, and invoke, in pursuance of a vow of long standing, the spirits of Crusoe and Columbus, who had knelt there before him. Then no doubt, as they returned by the harbour to integrate their room in the Great Southern, she would see the sun sink in the sea. How was it possible to give them her attention with such a prospect opening up before her? Oh well is thee, and happy shalt thou be.

Otto Olaf sang a little song. Mrs bboggs just sat, a big blank beldam, scarcely alive. Una struck the table sharply with a big pencil. When some measure of order had been restored, some little show of attention, she said, consulting her list:

'We have only five maids: the Clegg twins and the Purefoy triplets.'

This statement was not disputed. It seemed to Otto Olaf that five was a very respectable haul. It would have been considered so in his day.

'But we need nine' cried Una.

By good fortune a thought now presented itself to Mrs bboggs.

'My dear' she said, 'would not seven be ample?'

For two pins Una would have walked out of the conference.

'I think not' she said.

The idea! As though it were the wind-up of the football season.

'However' she added 'it is not my wedding.'

The ironical tone conveyed to this concession provoked Thelma to side with her mother for once. At no time indeed was this an easy matter, Mrs bboggs being almost as non-partisan as Pope Celestine the fifth. Dante would probably have disliked her on this account.

'I am all in favour' said Thelma 'of as few as is decent.'

'It's a very distinguished quorum' said Otto Olaf, 'more so even than nine.'

'As head maid' said Una 'I protest.'

Again Mrs bboggs came to the rescue. She had never been in such form.

'Then that leaves one' she said.

'What about Ena Nash?' said Thelma.

'Impossible' said Una. 'She reeks.'

'Then the McGillycuddy woman' said Otto Olaf.

Mrs bboggs sat up.

'I know of no McGillycuddy woman' said Una. 'Mother, do you know of any McGillycuddy woman?'

No, Mrs bboggs was completely in the dark. She and Una therefore began to wait indignantly for an explanation.

'Sorry' said Otto Olaf, 'no offence.'

'But who is the woman?' cried mother and daughter together.

'I spoke without thinking' said Otto Olaf.

Mrs bboggs was utterly nonplussed. How was it possible to name a woman without thinking? The thing was psychologically impossible. With mouth ajar and nostrils dilated she goggled psychological impossibilities at the offender.

'Hell roast the pair of you' he said in a sudden pet, 'I was only joking.'

Mrs bboggs, though still entirely at a loss, made up her mind in a flash to accept this explanation. Una was not in the least amused. In fact she was sorely tempted to wash her hands of the whole affair.

'I propose Alba Perdue' she said. It was really more a nomination than a proposal.

'That is her last word' observed Otto Olaf.

Alba Perdue, it may be remembered, was the nice little girl in A Wet Night. Thelma, whom Belacqua had favoured with his version of that half-remembered love, could scarcely dissemble her great satisfaction. When the turmoil of her blood had sufficiently abated she pronounced, in a voice just loud enough to be heard, this most depreciative hyperbole.

'I second that.'

Now it was Otto Olaf's turn to make enquiries.

'I understand' said Una who, unlike her father, could give a plain answer to a plain question, 'correct me, Thelma, if I am wrong, an old flame of the groom.'

'Then she won't act' said the simple Otto Olaf.

Even Mrs bboggs could not refrain from joining in the outburst of merriment that greeted this fatuity. Una in particular seemed certain to do herself an injury. She trembled and perspired in a most fearful manner.

'Oh my God!' she panted, 'won't act!'

But Nature takes care of her own and a loud rending noise was heard. Una stopped laughing and remained perfectly still. Her bodice had laid down its life to save hers.

Belacqua was so quiescent during the fortnight that preceded the ceremony that it almost seemed as though he were to suffer a complete metamorphosis. He had left all the arrangements to the discretion of Capper Quin, saying: 'Here is the money, do the best you can.'

But before being overtaken by this inertia, which proceeded partly from fatigue and partly no doubt from the need for self-purification, he had been kept busy in a number of ways: finding a usurer, redeeming the ring and searching among the hags for two to tally with Mr and Mrs bboggs in the interests of the nuptial jamboree. In the prosecution of this last duty Belacqua was called upon to sustain every kind of abusive denial and suffer Lucy's posthumous temperature to be thrown in his face, as though she were a bottle of white Burgundy. Until finally a female cousin, so remote as to be scarcely credible, and a kind of moot Struldbrug, to whom Belacqua's father had used to refer as 'dear old Jimmy the Duck', agreed to rise to the occasion. Hermione Näutzsche and James Skyrm were the names of these two deadbeats. Belacqua had not laid eyes on either of them since he was an infant prodigy.

Except for a short daily visit from Thelma, swallowed as being all in the game, Belacqua's retreat was undisturbed. The wedding gifts flowered in, not upon him, for he was friendless, but upon her, and she encouraged him day by day with the bulletin of their development.

She arrived one afternoon in a state of some excitement. Belacqua raised himself in the bed to be kissed, which he was with such unexpected voracity that he went weak before the end. Poor fellow, he had not been giving due attention to his meals.

'Your present is got' she said.

To Belacqua, who had been setting aside a portion of each day for polyglot splendours, this phrase came as a great shock. Perhaps the present would make him amends.

'It came this morning' she said.

'At what time exactly?' said Belacqua, easing his nerves in the usual sneer. 'That is most important.'

'What devil' said Thelma, her gaiety all gone, 'makes you so beastly?'

Ah, if he only knew.

'But it so happens' she said 'that I can tell you.'

Belacqua thought for a bit and then plumped for saying nothing.

'Because' she proceeded 'the first thing I did was to set it.'

The hideous truth dawned on his mind.

'Not a clock' he implored, 'don't say a grandfather clock.'

'The grandfather and mother' she did say 'of a period clock.'

He turned his face to the wall. He who of late years and with the approval of Lucy would not tolerate a chronometer of any kind in the house, for whom the local publication of the hours was six of the best on the brain every hour, and even the sun's shadow a torment, now to have this time-fuse deafen the rest of his days. It was enough to make him break off the engagement.

Long after she had gone he tossed and turned until the thought, like God appearing to a soul in hell, that he could always spike the monster's escapement and turn its death's-head to the wall, came in the morning with the canticle of the ring-doves. Then he slept.

What time Capper Quin was here, there and everywhere, attending to the interests of his principal. Conscious of his own shortcomings in a matter so far removed from the integrities of self-expression, he engaged, on the basis of a modest inverted commission, to aid him in this work, one Sproule, a lately axed jobber to a firm in the City, whose winning manner and familiarity with the shopping centres north of the river were beyond rubies. Bright and early on the fateful Saturday they met to buy the bouquets, the big one for the bride and seven nosegays.

'Mrs bboggs' said Hairy, 'ought we?'

'Ought we what?' said Sproule.

'I thought maybe a bloom' said Hairy.

'Superfoetation' said Sproule.

He led the way to a florist's off Mary Street. The proprietress, having just discovered among her stock an antirrhinum with the rudiment of a fifth stamen, was highly delighted.

'Oh, Mr Sproule sir' she exclaimed, 'would you believe it...'

'Good morning' said Sproule. 'One large orchid and seven of your best ox-eyes.'

Now Capper Quin, however unsuited to strike a bargain, was endowed with a sense of fitness, and one so exquisite indeed that he could make himself clear in its defence.

'On behalf of my client' he said 'I must insist on two orchids.'

'By all means' said Sproule. 'Make it three, make it a dozen.'

'Two' repeated Hairy.

'Two large orchids' said Sproule 'and seven of your best ox-eyes.' As though by magic wand the nine blooms appeared in her hand.

'Four lots' said Sproule, 'one, two, three and one with orchids.' Rapidly he equated addresses and consignments on a sheet of paper. 'So' he said, 'first thing.'

She now mentioned a sum that caused the buyer great amusement. He appealed to Hairy.

'Mr Quin' he said, 'do I wake or sleep?'

She not merely made good her figures but mentioned that she had to live. Sproule could not see the connexion. He pinched his cheek to make sure he was not in Nassau Street. 'My dear madam' he said, 'we do not have to live in Nassau Street.'

This thrust so weakened his adversary that she suffered him to place specie in her hand.

'Take this' he said, in a eucharistic voice, 'or leave it.'

The cold alloy in her hot palm, conjoined with the depression and the urge to live, determined the issue in Sproule's favour. Upon which the combatants shook hands with great heartiness. How could there be any question of rancour when both were fully satisfied of having obtained the victory?

Sproule, his duties at an end, received his commission in the Oval bar, where nothing would do him but that Hairy should toast his employer in gin and peppermint.

'Happy dawg' said Sproule. He had come unscathed through the Great War.

The hyperaesthesia of Hairy was so great that the mere fact of standing on licensed ground, without the least reference to its liberties, was of force sufficient to exhilarate him. Now therefore, under the influence of his situation, he dilated with splendid incoherence on the contradiction involved in the idea of a happy Belacqua and on the impertinence of desiring that he should derogate into such an anomaly.

'Fornication' he vociferated 'before the Shekinah.'

This observation was accompanied and graced by a spasm of such passionate repugnance that it was no less than an act of charity on the part of the ex-jobber, who was familiar with Boy Scouts and their ways and knew that he might never pass that way again, to substitute his empty glass for the bumper of his agitated companion.

In the bright street a bitter-sweet sorrow entered into Sproule, sweet at parting, bitter at the knowledge that his services were no longer required.

'Farewell' he said, flinging out his dreadful hand, 'may luck rise with you on the way.'

But Hairy was too full, too overcome by the fumes of his position, to shake, let alone reply. He stepped, as upon an Underground escalator, into the stream of pedestrians and was gone. Sproule raised his sad eyes to the sky and saw the day, its outstanding hours that could not be numbered, in the form of a beautiful Girl Guide galante, reclining among the clouds. She beckoned to him with her second finger, like one preparing a certificate in pianoforte, Junior Grade, at the Leinster School of Music. Closing his mind softly on this delicious vision, feeling it in his mind like a sponge of toilet vinegar on a fever, he advanced into the Oval towards it.

Whom should Hairy meet on the crest of the Metal Bridge but Walter Draffin, fresh from his effeminate ablutions and as spruce and keen as a new-ground hatchet in his miniature tails and stripes. The sun shone bright upon him, his languorous poll, for he carried his topper crown downward in his hand. The two gentlemen were on speaking terms.

'This is where I stand' said the little creature, with a sigh that made Hairy look nervously round for prisons and palaces, 'and watch the Liffey swim.'

'Blue-eyed cats' quoted the colossal Capper, for no other reason than that the phrase had been running in his mind and now here was a chance to discharge it on a wit, 'are always deaf.'

Walter smiled, he felt greatly pleased, he held up his little face to the kindly sun like a child to be kissed.

'The burrowing tucutucu' he answered 'is occasionally blind, but the mole is never sober.'

The mole is never sober. A profound mot. Hairy, having tried all he knew to say as much, hung his head, a gallant loser, consoled by the certitude that Walter would take the will for the deed. Poor Hairy, there was a great deal he understood, but he could not make this known in the absence of a battery of writing materials.

'That unspeakable invite' exclaimed Walter, 'of all things to be destitute of enjambment!'

He was confirmed in his initial misgiving by Hairy's having clearly no idea what he was talking about. There was nothing for it but to put it into his book. Walter's book was a long time in coming out because he refused to regard it as anything more than a mere dump for whatever he could not get off his chest in the ordinary way.

'So off you go' he said 'to attend your happy client, and I to buy myself a buttonhole.'

This, ensuing so soon upon mole and enjambment, brought Hairy's brain to the boil, and out of his mouth came the one word 'rose' like a big bubble.

'Blood-red and newly born' said Walter 'to aromatic pain. Eh?'

Hairy, with a sudden feeling that he was wasting his client's time and his own precarious energies on a kind of rubber Stalin, took his departure with a more than boorish abruptness, leaving Walter to enjoy the great central agency and hang out as it were his cowlick to air or dry. A passing humorist dropped a penny into the empty hat, it fell on the rich wadding without a sound, and so the joke was lost.

In Parliament Street a funeral passed and Hairy did not uncover. Many of the chief mourners, consoling themselves in no small measure with the reverence expressed by every section of the community, noticed with rage in their hearts that he did not, though to be sure they made no allusion to it at the time. Let this be a lesson to young men, strangers perhaps to sorrow, to uncover whenever a funeral passes, less in act of respect towards the defunct than in sympathetic acknowledgment of the survivors. One of these fine days Hairy will observe, from where he sits bearing up bravely behind the hearse in a family knot, a labourer let go of his pick with one hand, or gay dandy snatch both his out of his pockets, in a gesture of more value and comfort than a ton of lilies. Take the case of Belacqua, who ever since the commitment of his Lucy wears a hat, contrary to his inclination, on the off chance of his encountering a cortège.

The best man had received instructions to collect in Molesworth Street the Morgan, fast but noisy, lent for the period of the high-time journey by a friend of the bboggses. Needless to say some eejit had parked it so far up towards the arty end that luckless Hairy, coming from the west upon the stand after the usual Duke Street complications, hastening along the shady southern pavement because he felt there was not a moment to lose, was almost in despair of ever finding the solitary hind-wheel that he had been advised to look out for. He was much relieved to espy it at last, last but one or two in the row, but embarrassed also to remark a group made up of small boys, loafers and the official stand attendant gathered round passing judgment on the strange machine's design and performance. He kept his head none the less and examined the car, as he had been strictly enjoined to do, for any hymeneal insignia that might have been annexed, doubtless with the very best intentions, to its body, such as a boot, an inscription or other shameful badge. Satisfied that there were none, he hoisted his vast frame on board the light weight which thereupon reduced the expert comment of the by-standers, if we except the attendant who was most grave and attentive, to jeers and laughter, by rocking like a cockle-shell. Hairy, wondering what on earth to do next, sat blushing and hopeless at the controls. The general provisions for starting a motor engine were familiar to him, and these in every imaginable combination, he fruitlessly applied to that, exceptional presumably, fitted to the Morgan. The boys were most anxious to push, the loafers to give a tow, while the attendant could not be deterred from flooding the carburettor and swinging the engine, which started most perversely and unexpectedly with a backfire that broke the obliging fellow's arm. Hairy was so pressed for time that he hardened his heart to the consistence of an Uebermensch's, roared his engine and found himself abruptly, in a paroxysm of plunges and saccades, cutting the corner of Kildare Street under the prow of a bus, which happily did no more than remove the back number-plate and thus provide, not merely a neat instance of poetic justice, but the winged attendant with the nucleus of compensation.

All these little encounters and contretemps take place in a Dublin flooded with sunshine.

Belacqua had passed an excellent night, as he always did when he condescended to assign precise value to the content of his mind, no matter whether that were joy or sorrow, and did not awake when Hairy stalled the machine beneath his window on the cruel stroke of midday. Much liquor in secret the previous evening may have contributed to this torpor, but scarcely if at all; for many and many a time when footless, and simply because the forces in his mind would not resolve, he had tossed and turned like the Florence of Sordello and found all postures painful.

He opened his burning eyes on Hairy, rose, bathed, shaved and decked himself out, all in silence and without the least assistance. They plunged the packed bag in the well of the Morgan. Belacqua stood before the pier-glass.

'It's a small thing, Hairy' he said, and his voice, after so long silence, grated on his ear, 'separates lovers.'

'Not mountain chain' said Hairy.

'No, nor city ramparts' said Belacqua.

Hairy made a lunge of condolence at his companion, he simply could not help it, and was repulsed.

'Am I all right behind?' asked Belacqua.

'You know what it is' said Hairy, asserting thus and with a clarity quite unusual in him his independence and intolerance of all posterior aspects, 'you perish in your own plenty.'

Belacqua pressed apart his lips with his forefinger.

'If what I love' he said 'were only in Australia.'

Capper the faithful companion simply faded away, at least for the purposes of conversation.

'Whereas what I am on the look out for' said Belacqua, pursuing it would almost seem his train of thought, 'is nowhere as far as I can see.'

'Vobiscum' whispered Capper. 'Am I right?'

A cloud obscured the sun, the room grew dark, the light ebbed from the pier-glass and Belacqua, feeling his eyes moist, turned away from the blurred image of himself.

'Remember' he said, 'true of me now who have ceased to Charleston: Dum vivit aut bibit aut minxit. Take a note of it now.'

The Quaker's get!

Then driving through the City it occurred to him that an empty buttonhole would be the haporth of tar and no error. So he entered a flower-shop and came out with a purple tassel of veronica, fixed in the wrong lapel. Hairy stared. What startled him was not so much the breach of etiquette as the foolhardiness of getting married in a turned suit.

A pestilential hotel was their next stop. Hairy changed his clothes and looked more mangy king of beasts than ever. Belacqua lunched frugally on stout and scallions, scarcely the meal, one would have thought, for a man about to be married for the second time. However.

At the Church of Saint Tamar, pointed almost to the point of indecency, the maids, attired in glove-tight gossamer and sporting the awful ox-eyes, having just been joined by Mrs bboggs, who had chosen gauze and a bunch of omphalodes in her bosom, and Walter, very shaky and exalted, were massed in the porch when Morgante and Morgutte, to adopt the venomous reference of Una, not arm in arm but in single file, came forward. All but Walter were taken quite aback by the bridegroom's breath. Mrs bboggs buried her face (poor little Thelma!) in the omphalodes, the Cleggs turned scarlet in unison, the Purefoys crowded into a shade, while Una was only restrained by her hatred of anything in the nature of sacrilege from spitting it out. Miss Perdue found the smell rather refreshing. The cad and his faithful companion advanced to the chancel and took up their stand beside the gate, the latter to the right and a little to the rear, holding a hat in each hand.

The south pews were plentifully furnished with members and adherents of the bboggs clan, while those to the north were empty save for two grotesques, seated far apart: Jimmy the Duck Skyrm, an aged cretin, outrageous in pepper and salt, Lavalliere and pull-over, gnashing his teeth without ceasing at invisible spaghetti; and Hermione Näutzsche, a powerfully built nymphomaniac panting in black and mauve between shipped crutches. Her missing sexual hemisphere, despite a keen look out all her life long, had somehow never entered her orbit, and now, bursting as she was with chalk at every joint, she had no great hopes of being rounded off in that interesting sense. Little does she dream what a flurry she has set up in the

spirits of Skyrm, as he gobbles and mumbles the air at the precise
remove of enchantment behind her.

'Ecce' hissed Hairy, according to plan, and Belacqua's heart made
a hopeless dash against the wall of its box, the church suddenly
cruciform cage, the bulldogs of heaven holding the chancel, the
procession about to give tongue in the porch, the transepts culs-de-
sac. The organist darted into his loft like an assassin and set in
motion the various forces that could be relied on to mature in a
merry peal all in good time. Thelma, looking very striking and illegi-
timate in grey and green pieds de poule, split skirt and pique inser-
tions of negress pink, swept up the aisle on the right arm of Otto
Olaf, in whose head since leaving 55 a snatch had been churning and
did not now desert him:

> Drink a little at a time,
> Put water in your wine,
> Miss your glass when you can,
> And go off the first man.

Wise old Otto Olaf! He died in the end of a clot and left his cellar to
the cuckoo.

The maids, terminating in the curious deltoid formation of the
Alba, Mrs bboggs and Walter, took their speed from the bride and
their demeanour from the head-maid, with the result that their advance was at once rapid and sullen, for Una had become aware of an
uncontrollable and ill-placed dehiscence in the stuff of her gossamer.
The dread lest this should come to a head as she braced herself to
receive her foul little sister's gloves and bouquet, over and above an
habitual misanthropy aggravated by the occasion, had made her,
and hence her team of maids, appear as cross as two sticks. Always
excepting the Alba who, bating the old pain in the core of her vitals
that seemed to be a permanent part of her existence, could scarcely
have been more diverted had she been the bride herself instead of
the odd maid out. Also with Walter so close on her heels she was
kept busy.

Without going so far as to say that Belacqua felt God or Thelma
the sum of the Apostolic series, still there was in some indetermin-
ate way communicated to the solemnisation a kind or sort of mys-

tical radiance that Joseph Smith would have found touching. Belacqua passed the ring like a mouse belling the cat, with a quick prayer all on his own that the marriage knuckle of his love might so swell against the token and pledge as to spare her the pain of ever reading, inscribed on its inner periphery: Mens mea Lucia lucescit luce tua. His state of mind was so tense and complex at this stage (not to be wondered at when we consider all that he had gone through: the bereavement, obliging him to wear a hat at all seasons; the sweet and fierce pain of his passion for Miss bboggs; the long retreat in bed that had landed him in a nice marasmus; the stout and scallions; and now the sense of being cauterised with an outward and visible sign) that it might be likened to that of his dear departed Lucy listening pale and agog for the second incidence of

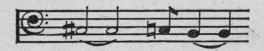

in the first movement of the Unbuttoned Symphony. Say what you will, you can't keep a dead mind down.

Talking of cats, Thelma remained throughout the service feline and inscrutable and was not at all incommoded by the famous viticultural passage which so abashed, or perhaps better angered, Belacqua that his platter face went from its native dingy to scarlet and back again through livid. Should he then avail himself of the first ... opportunity to sulphurate his bride and thus make sure? No, that would be doing the dirty on man's innocence. And make sure of what? Olives? Absurdity of the figure and all its harmonics like muscae volitantes provoked him to a copious scoff that would have put the kibosh on the sacrament altogether had it not been for the coolness and skill of the priest who covered as with a hand this coarseness with a collect.

Talking of hands, Thelma's right, as it danced through the find-the-lady sleights recommended in the liturgy, had quite bewitched the chancel. The curate swore he had never seen anything like it outside the Musée Rodin, it reminded the clerk of a Dürer cartoon and the priest of his incumbency, and it indicted Belacqua, tempest of stifled groans at having to produce anti-clockwise eyes and gestures for so long at a stretch, with Maupassant's scorching phrase: phylloxera of the spirit.

At length they had consented together beyond all possibility of cavil, the dearly beloved had for ever after held their peace and then let their cry come with a rush, and Otto Olaf's rendering of:

> Be present, awful Father!
> To give away this bride

had so moved the Sidneian heart of Skyrm that he transferred himself, for better for worse, into the pew where Hermione sat as on a thwart, and there, under cover of a kinsman's seasonable emotion, rooted and snuffled his way into her affections with a suilline avidity that can only have seemed horrible to any decent person not conversant with the phenomenon of crystallisation. The vestry was over, its signatures, duties and busses, and Mrs bboggs was back in 55, whipping the muslin off the Delikatessen, almost before the organist had regained control of his instrument. The Alba went with Walter in a taxi, Otto Olaf and Morgutte took a tram, the two grotesques never knew how they got there, while as for the maids, all but Una who wisely huddled on a cloak and cadged a lift, why they just floated on foot like brownies through the garish thoroughfares.

These are the little things that are so important.

To say that the drawing-room was thronged would be to put it mildly. It was stiff with guests. Otto Olaf found himself in that most painful of all possible positions, constrained to see his furniture, his loved ones, suffer and know himself helpless to relieve them.

There was something so bright and meaty about the assembly, something so whorled in its disposition with the procession loosely coiled in the midst waiting to move off, that Walter was slowly but surely put in mind of a Benozzo fresco and said so in his high-smelling voice to the Alba.

'Ass and all' she replied, with indescribable bitterness.

Una stamped her foot like a sheep and like sheep all present turned scared faces towards her. She had somehow contrived to consolidate and shore up her gossamer, but now she had fresh grounds for complaint, namely, that the newly-married couple, who should have been first home and in position for congratulations, had actually not yet turned up. Thus the action was brought to a dead halt. In its present headless condition the procession could not un-coil itself out through the door as arranged, and it was obvious that until the procession uncoiled itself there could be no relief for the congestion of casual ladies and gentlemen of which it was, so to speak, the mainspring. But let the truant pair appear and take their station and lo the press, as though by magic, would tick off merrily to its stand-up lunch. In the meantime, what a waste of good saliva!

'Raise me up Mr Quin' cried Una, in her anger throwing caution to the winds.

Hairy looked wildly at the bust of his partner, for so she was in pursuance of the regulations, they together forming – to vary the figure slightly – the fourth link of this nuptial hawser, in the im-mediate rear, that is, of Mrs bboggs and Skyrm, who in their turn surveyed the massive flitches of Hermione, sagging and flagging in her crutches as in a quicksand, and poor Otto Olaf, trembling in every limb – looking wildly at it for a point of purchase at once effective and respectful, some form of nelson that would not be too familiar, though for what purpose she desired to be raised he did not pause to inquire.

But before he could begin to make a mess of it in his flushing blushing panting ponderous way a great perturbation, dominated by the voice of Belacqua raised in abuse, made itself heard in the vestibule. This was they at last, but escorted by a pukkah Civic Guard of the highest rank compatible with duty and the stricken car-park attendant, as pale as a stone and clutching in his whole hand the damning number-plate.

Otto Olaf inserted his elbow in the eye of Hermione's crutch and released a dig. Having thus gained her attention he said, in a ruined whisper: 'My right lung is very weak.'

Hermione let a little pipe of terror.

'But my left lung' he vociferated 'is as sound as a bell.'

'I suppose' said Mrs bboggs to James Skyrm, whose facial paddles had begun to churn the air so fiercely that she feared lest he were meditating some gallant act on behalf of his kinswoman, 'I presume and I take it that Mr bboggs may do and say what he likes in his own home.'

James, on the matter being presented to him in this light, toed the line at once.

The tilted kepi of the attendant, its green band and gilt harp, and the clang beneath in black and white of his riotous hair and brow, so ravished Walter that he merely had to close his eyes to be back in Pisa. The powers of evocation of this Italianate Irishman were simply immense, and if his Dream of Fair to Middling Women, held up in the limae labor stage for the past ten or fifteen years, ever reaches the public, and Walter says it is bound to, we ought all be sure to get it and have a look at it anyway.

Belacqua reviled his captor and accuser with the utmost ferocity. Otto Olaf, then Capper, broke their ranks, the former to make a peace at all hazard, the later, with bursting heart, a clean breast. The attendant was very soon browbeaten into the admission that his injury had resulted, not from the ordinary exercise of his functions, not yet again from any act of solicited assistance, but purely and simply from his own excessive zeal, rooted beyond a shadow of doubt in greed.

A whip-round was made, and a small sum, on no account to be regarded as anything in the nature of an indemnity, subscribed charitably for his relief. This closed the incident.

'My heart bleeds for him' said Walter.

'Not at all' said the Alba, 'is he not insured?'

She had a sudden idea.

'See me home' she said to Walter.

Walter explained how he had been let in for a health, upon which, if the offer were still open, he would be more than happy to see her home. They would go one of the long ways round that he adored.

'I make no promises' said the Alba.

The lunch was a great disappointment to all and sundry – a few firkins of molasses and husks off the ice. Belacqua closed his eyes and saw, clearer than ever before, a beer-engine. The sweets were doled out and then Thelma refused to cut the cake. She was a very strange girl. Pressed hard by Una and Bridie she appealed to her husband. Her husband! His advice to her, quite frankly, when after great difficulty he discovered what she was talking about, was that it might be rather more gracious to cut the brute since all seemed so set on her doing so. Warming to his subject he urged her to hold out just a little longer, soon it would be all over. What had begun as a hurried and rather furtive aside now developed into a regular tête-à tête, and when at length Thelma turned to do the gracious thing she found the cake in bits. It had been dressed with orange blossoms. What few of these had escaped the oniromaniacs she gathered up and hid in her bosom. These she would lock up in the furthest recesses of a casket and cherish as long as she drew breath, these and her own two orchids and Belacqua's veronica, which spire of passionate devotion she had resolved to secure against all comers, vogue la galère! Time might pulverise these mementoes but at least their elements would belong to her for ever. She was a most strange girl.

Walter wiped his boots on the Aubusson of Otto Olaf's Empire ottoman, beat on his glass of Golden Guinea with his fizz-whisk for silence to fall and paid out his discourse, in a pawl-and-ratchet monotone than could never be unsaid, as follows:

'It is on record that a lady member of the Lower House, and feme covert what is more, rose to her feet, those feet – for she was of Dublin stock – that Swift, rebuking the women of this country for their disregard of Shank's mare, described as being fit for nothing better than to be laid aside, and declared: "I would rather commit adultery than suffer one drop of intoxicating liquor to pass my lips." To which a gross baker, returned in the Labour interest, reported: "Wouldn't we all rather do that, Maam?" '

This opening passage was rather too densely packed to gain the general suffrage. On Otto Olaf it took effect some five minutes later, causing him to laugh in a helpless and hysterical manner. The sight of Walter, ranging to and fro on his fantastic upholstery as though he were caged or contesting an election, had capsized his whole nervous system and his heart was filling up rapidly with evil and madness.

' "Il faut marcher avec son temps" said a Deputy of the extreme Right. "Cela dépend" answered Briand in his sepulchral sneer "dans quoi il marche." So do not heckle me, Herrschaften, because that would about finish me.'

He dropped his head, like a pelican after a long journey, pricked up the ears of his fearful moustache and shuffled and shifted his feet like one surprised in a dishonourable course of action. 'He is out of his head' said the chief of the ill-intentioned ladies. Otto Olaf sidled up to the dumb-waiter. Una sat down with great ostentation on a pouf. 'Let me know when he starts' she said. Thelma's eyes were darting this way and that in search of orange-blossom, Belacqua was watching Thelma and the Alba was watching him. James and Hermione, emboldened by the molasses, were trying themselves on before a Regence trumeau. Mrs bboggs was manoeuvring for a vantage-ground that would bring both husband and lover into her field of vision. The usual precautionary plain-clothes man, standing head and shoulders out of the ruck, was reading his paper. Two splendid mixers found themselves adjacent. 'Drunk' said the first, 'well lit' agreed the second, and they exchanged a long look of intelligence.

In fairness to Walter it must be said that he was far from being penetrate with this hangdog façade, behind which all was mercy-seat al fresco and Shekinah and himself, in the smartest mail, having his wounds dressed by the Alba-Morgen and looking through the orchards at the sun setting awkwardly in the blue shallows. Coming to with a start, shedding his cloak of dejection, he spoke the first words that he came across in his head:

> 'Semper ibi juvenis cum virgine, nulla senectus
> Nullaque vis morbi, nullus dolor. . . .'

Mrs bboggs, having already trembled to hear the belated chuckling of Otto Olaf and to observe his stealthy movements as he called in all the castle puddings on the dumb-waiter, was hardly surprised when he now opened rapid fire on his enemy with these. But Walter was able to block such trivial missiles, even caught one and ate it, while the old man's strength, and with it his rage was soon spent. His arteries began to fray, with the fatal result as aforesaid, from this moment.

'I raise this glass' said Walter, extending it low down and a little to the left before him like a buckler, 'this glorious bumper, on behalf of those present and the many prevented by age, sickness, infirmity or previous engagement from being with us, to you, dearest Thelma, whom we all love, and to you, Mr Shuah, who Thelma loving and being loved of her we all love too I feel sure, now on the threshold of your bliss, and to such and so many consummations, earthly and other, as you have in mind.'

He plied the whisk, dealt himself a slow uppercut with the glass, and drank.

'I close these eyes' he proceeded, fixing them on Mrs bboggs and returning the glass to its base, 'and I see them in that memorable island, Avalon, Atlantis, Hesperides, Ui Breasail, I don't insist, lapped in the Siamese haecceity of puffect love, revelling in the most delightful natural surroundings. Oh may that star, that radiant radical of their desire, not of mine, my friends, nor yet of yours, for no two stars, as Saint Paul tells us, are on a par in the matter of glory, delight them without ceasing with legitimate inflexions!' He unleashed what was left of the glorious bumper. 'To Hymen's gracious mussy and protection we commit them, now, henceforth and for evermore. Slainte.'

This was the end of Walter's speech, and a very good end for such a bad speech everyone felt it to be; but as he remained upright on the ottoman in a rapt and suspended pose, drinking in the plaudits, Belacqua assumed that there was some yet to come and so was startled to hear the voice of Una, whom the least semblance of procrastination invariably threw into the most dreadful passion, calling on him petulantly to do the needful: 'Now Mr Shuah, now then Mr Shuah, we're waiting on yer Mr Shuah.' This sordid hitch caused his acknowledgment to be rather less cordial than he had intended. He made it from where he stood, in the white voice of which he was a master:

'I have to thank: Miss bboggs, who henceforward may be so addressed without the least ambiguity, for her as always timely reminder; Mr Draffin, for his kind torrents of meiosis; Mr and Mrs small double bee, for their Bounty; the Maids, with special reference to Belle-Belle their leader, for their finely calculated offices this day, something more than merely buttress and less than vis a tergo; the Skyrm and Nāutzsche, who I am glad to see have not yet done rising to the occasion; my faithful friend and best of men, Tiny Hairy Capper Quin, tipping the scale, day in day out, for me and for many, whose spiritual body is by now I feel confident a fait accompli; the entire Church staff; the Abbé Gabriel; as many, in fine, as have found the time to witness and acclaim, in how small a way soever, this instant of the whirligig. Eleleu. Jou Jou.'

A student of Plutarch found himself rubbing shoulders with a physicist of the modern school.

'There you have him' said the first 'in a nutshell.'

'This bivalve world' said the other.

Whatever small chance these words of Belacqua might have had of giving satisfaction was more than cancelled by his having been observed, in a dumb-show portmanteau of Selah and sigh of relief, to check off on his fingers each acknowledgment as it was made. Thelma marched to the door in an atmosphere of silence and shock, opened it and closed it behind her, which expression of independence rather cut the ground away from under Una, who had planned to sit down with a bang on the pouf, just at the moment when her services were obviously most needed, and thus put an open slight on the bride.

Hairy on the other hand, faithful to the last to his commission, reported smartly for duty.

'Slip out quick' said Belacqua 'and run her behind into the lane off Denmark Street.'

The guests were now adjourning stiffly to the drawing-room, Walter and Otto Olaf polarised in bitter tig about the person of the Alba, Otto Olaf being it, while Hermione and James, he propelling her in a tomb-deep armchair on casters, closed the recession. This grotesque equipage was brought to a standstill in the passage in consequence of the passenger's putting her feet on the ground, whether from coquetry or fatigue, we leave it to the reader to determine.

'My crutches Jim' she said.

Jim went back for the crutches, Walter took sanctuary with Hermione, the Alba sent Otto Olaf flying, Jim came back with the sweeps, Hermione got them under her somehow, Walter rejoined the Alba. They remained all four quietly where they were, in the passage, discussing ways and means, severally first, then, when their interests were overheard to coincide, together. Four heads are better than two, eight than four, and so on.

After a fairly decent interval Belacqua excused himself just for a moment (as he did, it may be remembered, to the Poet in the Grosvenor), left the room, sprang up the stairs, caught up his bride like a Cossack and conveyed her by clandestine ways down to the garden that lay behind the house. He opened the wicket into the lane with the key that his love had fondly hoped would facilitate his suit in its early stages, and in another moment they had been clear of the abhorred premises when the sound of a broken-winded hue in the garden caused him to turn back. This proceeded from that irrepressible quartet, Hermione, the Alba, Walter and James, perspiring, suppliant, making their getaway.

Belacqua stood like a stock at gaze, with an overwhelming sense that all this would happen to him again, in a dream or subsequent existence. Then he stepped to the one side, Thelma to the other, of the wicket, Caudine exit, saying to himself, as he watched the fugitives storm the postern like women boarding a tram: 'It is right that they who are loved should live.' It was from this moment that he used to date in after years his crucial loss of interest in himself, as in a grape beyond his grasp.

But the alarm had been given, faces sprang up in the windows, Una began to scream havoc fit to burst, the mixers and the plainclothes man came plunging up the garden in the van of pursuit. Belacqua threw them a tub in the form of Hairy, locked the wicket on the outside and committed himself and his wife to the Morgan, fast but noisy.

As for the other four, they did not feel safe until they reached the Cappella Lane, superb cenotheca, in Charlemont House. Nobody would ever think of looking for them there.

Lucy was atra cura in the dicky the best part of the way down to Galway.

They all stopped for a drink. Thelma, as ever on his wrong side, began to insist that she was Mrs Shuah, making his little heart go pit-a-pat. He turned a face that she had never seen upon her.

'Do you ever hear tell of a babylan?' he said.

Now Thelma was a brave girl.

'A what did you say?' she said.

Belacqua went to the trouble of spelling the strange word.

'Never' she said. 'What is it? Something to eat?'

'Oh' he said 'you're thinking of a baba.'

'Well then' she said.

His eyes were parched, he closed them and saw, clearer than ever before, the mule, up to its knees in mire, and astride its back a beaver, flogging it with a wooden sword.

But she was not merely brave, she was discreet as well.

'Your veronica' she said 'that I wanted so much, where is it gone?'

He clapped his hand to the place. Alas! The tassel had drooped, wormed its stem out of the slit, fallen to the ground and been trodden underfoot.

'Gone west' he said.

They went further.

THE
SMERALDINA'S
BILLET DOUX

Bel Bel my own bloved, allways and for ever mine!!

Your letter is soked with tears death is the onely thing. I had been crying bitterly, tears! tears! tears! and nothing els, then your letter cam with more tears, after I had read it ofer and ofer again I found I had ink spots on my face. The tears are rolling down my face. It is very early in the morning, the sun is riseing behind the black trees and soon that will change, the sky will be blue and the trees a golden brown, but there is one thing that dosent change, this pain and thos tears. Oh! Bel I love you terrible, I want you terrible, I want your body your soft white body Nagelnackt! My body needs you so terrible, my hands and lips and breasts and everything els on me, sometimes I find it very hard to keep my promise but I have kept it up till now and will keep on doing so until we meet again and I can at last have you, at last be the Geliebte. Whitch is the greater: the pain of being away from eachother, or the pain of being with eachother, crying at eachother beauty? I supose the last is the greater, otherwise we would of given up all hope of ever being anything els but miserable.

I was at a grand Film last night, first of all there wasent any of the usual hugging and kissing, I think I have never enjoyed or felt so sad at a Film as at that one, Sturm uber Asien, if it comes to Dublin you must go and see it, the same Regie as Der Lebende Leichnam, it was realey something quite diffrent from all other Films, nothing to do with Love (as everybody understands the word) no silly girls makeing sweet faces, black lakes and grand Landschaften. Comeing home there was a new moon, it looked so grand ofer the black trees that it maid me cry. I opened my arms wide and tryed to imagine that you were lieing against my breasts and looking up at me like you did those moonlight nights when we walked together under the big chestnut trees with the stars shineing through the branches.

I met a new girl, very beautiful, pitch black hairs and very pale, she onely talks Egyptian. She told me about the man she loves, at present he is in Amerika far away in some lonely place and wont be back for the next three years and cant writ to her because there is no post office where he is staying and she onely gets a letter every 4 months, imagine if we only got a letter from eachother every 4 months what sort of state wc would be in by now, the poor girl I am very sorry for her. We went to a 5 o'clock tea dance, it was rather boreing but quite amuseing to see the people thinking of nothing but what they have on and the men settling their tyes every 5 minutes. On the way home I suddenly got in to a terrible state of sadness and woulden say a word, of course they were rageing with me, at the moment I dident care a dam, when I got in to the bus I got out a little Book and pencil and wrot down 100 times: Bloved Bloved Bloved Bel Bel Bel, I felt as if I never longed so much in my life for the man I love, to be with him, with him. I want you so much in every sense of the word, you and onely you. After I got out of the bus and was walking down the street I yelled out wahnsinnig! wahnsinnig! wahnsinnig! Frau Schlank brought down your sock and that made me cry more than ever. I don't think I will send it to you, I will put it in to the drawer with your sweet letter. I had allso a letter from a man who asked me to go out with him to dance on Saturday evening, I sopose I will go. I know my bloved dosent mind and it makes the time go round quicker, the man is a bit of a fool but dances quite well and is the right hight for me. A flirt is very amuseing but shouldent go further than that.

Then I met the old man with the pipe and he told me I had a blue letter and then the fat man with the keys in the passage and he said Grüss Gott but I dident hear him.

Soon I will be counting the hours untill I can go to the station and find you amongst the crowded platform but I dont think I will be able to wear my grey costume if it is too cold and then I will have to wear Mammy furcoat. You will be by me on the 23th wont you Bel, my Bel with the beautiful lips and hands and eyes and face and everything that is on you, and now with your poor sore face it would make no difference. Two more weeks of agony pain and sadness! 14 more days oh! God and thos sleepless nights!!! How long? How long?

I had a very queer dream last night about you and me in a dark forest, we were lieing together on a path, when sudenly you changed in to a baby and dident know what love was and I was trying to tell you that I loved you more than anything on earth but you dident understand and wouldent have anything to do with me but it was all a dream so it dosent count. There is no object in my trying to tell you how much I love you because I will never succeed, I know that for sirten. Is he the man I have allways been looking for? Yes! but then why cant he give that what I have been longing for for the last 6 months? I often wonder what is on you that makes me love you so greatly. I love you uber alles in dieser Welt, mehr als alles auf Himmel, Erde und Hölle. One thing I thank God for that our love is so vast. I often wonder who I am to thank that you are born and that we met, I sopose I better not start trying to find out whose fault it is that you are born. It comes back to the same thing, and that is, that I onely know ONE THING and that is that I LOVE YOU AND I AM ALLWAYS YOUR SMERALDINA and that is the onely thing that matters most in our life YOU LOVE ME AND ARE ALL-WAYS MY BEL.

Analiese is hacking round on the piano and there is no peace so I will stop. Now I am going to go on reading my Book called Die Grosse Liebe and then perhaps I will try and struggel through the Beethoven sonate, it is the onely thing that can take me away from my misery, I love playing quietly to myself in the evenings it give me such a rest.

Bel! Bel! Bel! your letter has just come! Even if you cease to be all and allways mine!!! Oh! God how could you ever say such a thing, for lord sake dont!!! for god sake dont ever suggest such a thing again! I just berry my head in my hands and soke your letter with tears ... Bel! Bel! how could you ever doubt me? Meine Ruh ist hin mein Herz ist schwer ich finde Sie nimmer und nimmer mehr. (Goethes Faust.) Lord Lord Lord for god sake tell me strate away what agsactly I have done. Is everything indiffrent to you? Evedintly you cant be bothered with a goat like me. If I don't stop writing you wont be able to read this letter because it will be all ofer tears. Bel! Bel! my love is so vast that when I am introduced to some young man and he starts doing the polite I get a quivver all ofer. I know what I am lifeing for, your last letter is allways on my breast when I wake up in the morning and see the sun rise. Ich seh Dich nicht mehr Tränen hindern mich! My God! my true dog! my baby!

I must get a new nib, this old pen is gone to the dogs, I cant writ with it any more, it is the one I got from Wollworth so you can imagine how good it must be.

Mammy wanted me to go out for a walk this afternoon, but I hate walking, I get so tired putting one foot delibertely in front of the other. Do you remember last summer (of course he dose) and how lovely it was lieing hearing the bees summing and the birds singing, and the big butterfly that cam past, it looked grand, it was dark brown with yellow spots and looked so beautiful in the sun, and my body was quite brown all ofer and I dident feel the cold any more. Now the snow is all melted and the wood is as black as ever and the sky is allways grey except in the early morning and even then one can onely see spots of red between the black clouds.

My hairs are freshily washed and I have a bit more energie than usual but still feel very passiv. For god sake dont overdo yourself and try and not get drunk again, I mean in that way that makes you sick.

We cam home in the bus this evening but we dident go that way through the fields with all the little paths because the big road was mended. Mammy allways asks after you. She says the time is flying, it will be no time untill Xmas and she says she hopes Frau Holle makes her bed ofen. I heard her saying to Daddy, I wonder how it is that Ivy and Bill get on my nerves when they go on to-gether and Smerry and Bel never did. She ment when we are sitting on eachother knee and so on, I think it is because the love between Ivy and Bill is not real, there allways seems to be some sort of affection about it.

I curse the old body all day asswell because I have some dam thing on my leg so that I can bearly walk, I dont know what it is or how it got there but it is there and full of matter to hell with it.

To-day is one of the days when I see everything more clearer than ever and I am sure everything will go right in the end.
Der Tag wird kommen und die stille
NACHT!!!

I dont genau know when but if I dident think so I would cullaps with this agony, thes terrible long dark nights and onely your image to console me. I like the little white statue so much and am longing for the day when you and I will be standing like that and not haveing to think that there is somebody outside that can come in any minute.

Arschlochweh is married and gone to the Schweiz with his wife. You ask me to give you a taske. I think I have gived you a big enough a taske. I am longing to see the 'thing' you wrot about my 'beauty' (as you call it) I must say (without wanting any complements) I can't see anything very much to writ about except the usual rot men writ about women.

Darling Bel I must stop. My bed is lonely without me and your photograph is waiting to be kissed so I better give them both peace. Soon it will all take an end, you will be by me and will feel that marvellous pain again that we did in the dark mountains and the big black lake blow and will walk in the fields covered with cowslips and Flieder and will hold once more in your arms

your own sad bloved
SMERALDINA

P.S. One day nearer to the silent Night! ! !

YELLOW

THE NIGHT-NURSE bounced in on the tick of five and turned on the light. Belacqua waked feeling greatly refreshed and eager to wrestle with this new day. He had underlined, as quite a callow boy, a phrase in Hardy's Tess, won by dint of cogging in the Synod: When grief ceases to be speculative, sleep sees her opportunity. He had manipulated that sentence for many years now, emending its terms, as joy for grief, to answer his occasions, even calling upon it to bear the strain of certain applications for which he feared it had not been intended, and still it held good through it all. He waked with it now in his mind, as though it had been there all the time he slept, holding that fragile place against dreams.

The nurse brought a pot of tea and a glass of strong salts on a tray.

'Pfui!' exclaimed Belacqua.

But the callous girl preferred to disregard this.

'When are they doing me?' he asked.

'You are down for twelve' she said.

Down...!

She took herself off.

He drank the salts and two cups of tea and be damned to the whole of them. Then of course he was wide awake, poor fellow. But what cared he, what cared saucy Belacqua? He switched off the lamp and lay back on his back in this the darkest hour, smoking.

Carry it off as he might, he was in a dreadful situation. At twelve sharp he would be sliced open – zeep! – with a bistoury. This was the idea that his mind for the moment was in no fit state to entertain. If this Hunnish idea once got a foothold in his little psyche in its present unready condition, topsy-turvy after yesterday's debauch of anxiety and the good night's sleep coming on top of that, it would be annihilated. The psyche, not the idea, which was precisely the reverse of what he wished. For himself, to do him justice, he did not care. His mind might cave in for all he cared, he was tired of the old bastardo. But the unfortunate part of it was that this would appear in his behaviour, he would scream and kick and bite and scratch when they came for him, beg for execution to be stayed and perhaps even wet the bed, and what a reflection on his late family that would be! The grand old family Huguenot guts, he could not do the dirty on them like that. (To say nothing of his natural anxiety to be put to rights with as little fuss as possible.)

My sufferings under the anaesthetic, he reflected, will be exquisite, but I shall not remember them.

He dashed out his cigarette and put on the lamp, this not so much for the company of the light as in order to postpone daybreak until he should feel a little more sure of himself. Daybreak, with its suggestion of a nasty birth, he could not bear. Downright and all as he was, he could not bear the sight of this punctilious and almost, he sometimes felt, superfluous delivery. This was mere folly and well he knew it. He tried hard to cure himself, to frighten or laugh himself out of this weakness, but to no avail. He would grow tired and say to himself: I am what I am. That was the end of all his meditations and endeavours: I am what I am. He had read the phrase somewhere and liked it and made it his own.

But God at least was good, as He usually is if we only know how to take Him, in this way, that six hours separated him (Belacqua) from the ordeal, six hours were allotted to him in which to make up his mind, as a pretty drab her face for an enemy. His getting the fleam in the neck, his suffering the tortures of the damned while seeming to slumber as peacefully as a little child, were of no consequence, as hope saved they were not, so long as his mind were master of the thought of them. What he had to do, and had with typical slackness put off doing till the last moment, was to arrange a hot reception in his mind for the thought of all the little acts of kindness that he was to endure before the day was out. Then he would be able to put a good face on it. Otherwise not. Otherwise he would bite, scratch, etc., when they came for him. Now the good face was all that concerned him, the bold devil-may-care expression. (Except of course that he was also anxious to be made well with the least possible ado.) He did not pause to consider himself in this matter, the light that the coming ordeal would shed on his irrevocable self, because he really was tired of that old bastardo. No, his whole concern was with other people, the lift-boy, nurses and sisters, the local doc coming to put him off, the eminent surgeon, the handy man at hand to clean up and put the bits into the incinerator, and all the friends of his late family, who would ferret out the whole truth. It did not matter about him, he was what he was. But these outsiders, the family guts and so on and so forth, all these things had to be considered.

An asthmatic in the room overhead was coughing his heart up. God bless you, thought Belacqua, you make things easier for me. But when did the unfortunate sleep? During the day, the livelong day, through the stress of the day. At twelve sharp he would be sound, or, better again, just dozing off. Meantime he coughed, as Crusoe laboured to bring his gear ashore, the snugger to be.

Belacqua made a long arm and switched off the lamp. It threw shadows. He would close his eyes, he would bilk the dawn in that way. What were the eyes anyway? The posterns of the mind. They were safer closed.

If only he were well-bred, or failing that, plucky. Blue blood or game-cock! Even if he lived in his mind as much as was his boast. Then he need not be at all this pains to make himself ready. Then it would only be a question of finding a comfortable position in the strange bed, trying to sleep or reading a book, waiting calmly for the angelus. But he was an indolent bourgeois poltroon, very talented up to a point, but not fitted for private life in the best and brightest sense, in the sense to which he referred when he bragged of how he furnished his mind and lived there, because it was the last ditch when all was said and done. But he preferred not to wait till then, he fancied it might be wiser to settle down there straight away and not wait till he was kicked into it by the world, just at the moment maybe when he was beginning to feel at home in the world. He could no more go back into his heart in that way than he could keep out of it altogether. So now there was nothing for it but to lie on his back in the dark, and exercise his talent. Unless of course he chose to distress the friends of his late family (to say nothing of perhaps jeopardising the cure for which the friends of his late family were paying). But he had too much of the grocer's sense of honour for that. Rather than have that happen he would persist with his psyche, he would ginger up his little psyche for the occasion.

Poor Belacqua, he seems to be having a very dull irksome morning, preparing for the fray in this manner. But he will make up for it later on, there is a good time coming for him later on, when the doctors have given him a new lease of apathy.

What were his tactics in this crisis?

In a less tight corner he might have been content to barricade his mind against the idea. But this was at the best a slipshod method, since the idea, how blatant an enemy soever and despite the strictest guard, was almost certain to sidle in sooner or later under the skirts of a friend, and then the game was up. Still, in the ordinary run of adversity, he would doubtless have bowed to his natural indolence and adopted such a course, he would have been content merely to think of other things and hope for the best. But this was no common or garden fix, he was properly up against it this time, there could be no question of half-measures on this melancholy occasion.

His plan therefore was not to refuse admission to the idea, but to keep it at bay until his mind was ready to receive it. Then let it in and pulverise it. Obliterate the bastard. He ground his teeth in the bed. Flitter the fucker, tear it into pieces like a priest. So far so good. But by what means. Belacqua ransacked his mind for a suitable engine of destruction.

At this crucial point the good God came to his assistance with a phrase from the paradox of Donne: Now among our wise men, I doubt not but many would be found, who would laugh at Heraclitus weeping, none which would weep at Democritus laughing. This was a godsend and no error. Not the phrase as a judgment, but its terms, the extremes of wisdom that it rendered to Belacqua. It is true that he did not care for these black and white alternatives as a rule. Indeed he even went so far as to hazard a little paradox on his own account, to the effect that between contraries no alternation was possible. But was it the moment for a man to be nice? Belacqua snatched eagerly at the issue. Was it to be laughter or tears? It came to the same thing in the end, but which was it to be now? It was too late to arrange for the luxury of both. Now in a moment he

would fill his mind with one or other of these two orders of rays,
shall we say ultra-red and ultra-violet, and prepare to perforate his
adversary.

Really, thought Belacqua, I cannot remember having ever spent a
more dreary morning; but needs must, that was a true saying, when
the devil drives.

At this all-important juncture of his delirium Belacqua found
himself blinking his eyes rapidly, a regular nictation, so that little
flaws of dawn gushed into his mind. This had not been done with
intent, but when he found that it seemed to be benefiting him in
some curious way he kept it up, until gradually the inside of his
skull began to feel sore. Then he desisted and went back to the
dilemma.

Here, as indeed at every crux of the enterprise, he sacrificed his
sense of what was personal and proper to himself to the desirability
of making a certain impression on other people, an impression almost of gallantry. He must efface himself altogether and do the
little soldier. It was this paramount consideration that made him
decide in favour of Bim and Bom, Grock, Democritus, whatever you
are pleased to call it, and postpone its dark converse to a less public
occasion. This was an abnegation if you like, for Belacqua could not
resist a lachrymose philosopher and still less when, as was the
case with Heraclitus, he was obscene at the same time. He was in
his element in dingy tears and luxuriously so when these were furnished by a pre-Socratic man of acknowledged distinction. How often
had he not exclaimed, skies being grey: 'Another minute of this and
I consecrate the remnant of my life to Heraclitus of Ephesus, I shall
be that Delian diver who, after the third or fourth submersion,
returns no more to the surface!'

But weeping in this charnel-house would be misconstrued. All
the staff, from matron to lift-boy, would make the mistake of
ascribing his tears, or, perhaps better, his tragic demeanour, not to
the follies of humanity at large which of course covered themselves,
but rather to the tumour the size of a brick that he had on the back
of his neck. This would be a very natural mistake and Belacqua was
not blaming them. No blame attached to any living person in this
matter. But the news would get round that Belacqua, so far from
grinning and bearing, had piped his eye, or had been on the point of

doing so. Then he would be disgraced and, by extension, his late family also.

So now his course was clear. He would arm his mind with laughter, laughter is not quite the word but it will have to serve, at every point, then he would admit the idea and blow it to pieces. Smears, as after a gorge of blackberries, of hilarity, which is not quite the word either, would be adhering to his lips as he stepped smartly, ohne Hast aber ohne Rast, into the torture-chamber. His fortitude would be generally commended.

How did he proceed to put this plan into execution?

He has forgotten, he has no use for it any more.

The night-nurse broke in upon him at seven with another cup of tea and two cuts of toast.

'That's all you'll get now' she said.

The impertinent slut! Belacqua very nearly told her to work it up.

'Did the salts talk to you?' she said.

The sick man appraised her as she took his temperature and pulse. She was a tight trim little bit.

'They whispered to me' he said.

When she was gone he thought what an all but flawless brunette, so spick and span too after having been on the go all night, at the beck and call of the first lousy old squaw who let fall her book or could not sleep for the roar of the traffic in Merrion Row. What the hell did anything matter anyway!

Pale wales in the east beyond the Land Commission. The day was going along nicely.

The night-nurse came back for the tray. That made her third appearance, if he was not mistaken. She would very shortly be relieved, she would eat her supper and go to bed. But not to sleep. The place was too full of noise and light at that hour, her bed a refrigerator. She could not get used to this night-duty, she really could not. She lost weight and her little face became cavernous. Also it was very difficult to arrange anything with her fiancé. What a life!

'See you later' she said.

There was no controverting this. Belacqua cast about wildly for a reply that would please her and and do him justice at the same

time. Au plaisir was of course the very thing, but the wrong language. Finally he settled on I suppose so and discharged it at her in
a very half-hearted manner, when she was more than half out of the
door. He would have been very much better advised to let it alone
and say nothing.

While he was still wasting his valuable time cursing himself for a
fool the door burst open and the day-nurse came in with a mighty
rushing sound of starched apron. She was to have charge of him by
day. She just missed being beautiful, this Presbyterian from Aberdeen. Aberdeen!

After a little conversation obiter Belacqua let fall casually, as
though the idea had only just occurred to him, whereas in fact it
had been tormenting him insidiously for some little time:

'Oh nurse the W.C. perhaps it might be as well to know.'

Like that, all in a rush, without any punctuation.

When she had finished telling him he knew roughly where the
place was. But he stupidly elected to linger on in the bed with his
uneasy load, codding himself that it would be more decent not to
act incontinent on intelligence of so intimate a kind. In his anxiety
to give colour to this pause he asked Miranda when he was being
done.

'Didn't the night-nurse tell you' she said sharply, 'at twelve.'

So the night-nurse had split. The treacherous darling!

He got up and set out, leaving Miranda at work on the bed. When
he got back she was gone. He got back into the made bed.

Now the sun, that creature of habit, shone in through the window.

A little Aschenputtel, gummy and pert, skipped in with sticks and
coal for the fire.

'Morning' she said.

'Yes' said Belacqua. But he retrieved himself at once. 'What a
lovely room' he exclaimed 'all the morning sun.'

No more was needed to give Aschenputtel his measure.

'Very lovely' she said bitterly 'right on me fire.' She tore down the
blind. 'Putting out me good fire' she said.

That was certainly one way of looking at it.

'I had one old one in here' she said 'and he might be snoring but
he wouldn't let the blind down.'

Some old put had crossed her, that was patent.

'Not for God' she said 'so what did I do?' She screwed round on her knees from building the fire. Belacqua obliged her.

'What was that?' he said.

She turned back with a chuckle to her task.

'I block it with a chair' she said 'and his shirt over the back.'

'Ha' exclaimed Belacqua.

'Again he'd be up' she exulted 'don't you know.' She laughed happily at the memory of this little deception. 'I kep it off all right' she said.

She talked and talked and poor Belacqua, with his mind unfinished, had to keep his end up. Somehow he managed to create a very favourable impression.

'Well' she said at last, in an indescribable sing-song 'g'bye now. See you later.'

'That's right' said Belacqua.

Aschenputtel was engaged to be married to handy Andy, she had been for years. Meantime she gave him a dog's life.

Soon the fire was roaring up the chimney and Belacqua could not resist the temptation to get up and sit before it, clad only in his thin blue 100,000 Chemises pyjamas. The coughing aloft had greatly abated since he first heard it. The man was gradually settling down, it did not require a Sherlock Holmes to realise that. But on the grand old yaller wall, crowding in upon his left hand, a pillar of higher tone, representing the sun, was spinning out its placid deiseal. This dribble of time, thought Belacqua, like sanies into a bucket, the world wants a new washer. He would draw the blind, both blinds.

But he was foiled by the entry of the matron with the morning paper, this, save the mark, by way of taking his mind off it. It is impossible to describe the matron. She was all right. She made him nervous the way she flung herself about.

Belaqua turned on the flow:

'What a lovely morning' he gushed 'a lovely room, all the morning sun.'

The matron simply disappeared, there is no other word for it. The woman was there one moment and gone the next. It was extraordinary.

The theatre sister came in. What a number of women there seemed to be in this place! She was a great raw chateaubriant of a woman, like the one on the Wincarnis bottle. She took a quick look at his neck.

'Pah' she scoffed 'that's nothing.'

'Not at all' said Belacqua.

'Is that the lot?'

Belacqua did not altogether care for her tone.

'And a toe' he said 'to come off, or rather portion of a toe.'

'Top' she guffawed 'and bottom.'

There was no controverting this. But he had learnt his lesson. He let it pass.

This woman was found to improve on acquaintance. She had a coarse manner, but she was exceedingly gentle. She taught all her more likely patients to wind bandages. To do this well with the crazy little hand-windlass that she provided was no easy matter. The roll would become fusiform. But when one got to know the humours of the apparatus, then it could be coaxed into yielding the hard slender spools, perfect cylinders, that delighted her. All these willing slaves that passed through her hands, she blandished each one in turn. 'I never had such tight straight bandages' she would say. Then, just as the friendship established on this basis seemed about to develop into something more — how shall I say? — substantial, the patient would all of a sudden be well enough to go home. Some malignant destiny pursued this splendid woman. Years later, when the rest of the staff was forgotten, she would drift into the mind. She marked down Belacqua for the bandages.

Miranda came back, this time with the dressing-tray. That voluptuous undershot cast of mouth, the clenched lips, almost bocca romana, how had he failed to notice it before? Was it the same woman?

'Now' she said.

She lashed into the part with picric and ether. It beat him to understand why she should be so severe on his little bump of amativeness. It was not septic to the best of his knowledge. Then why this severity? Merely on the off chance of its coming in for the fag-end of a dig? It was very strange. It had not even been shaved. It jutted out under the short hairs like a cuckoo's bill. He trusted it

would come to no harm. Really he could not afford to have it cur-
tailed. His little bump of amativeness.

When his entire nape was as a bride's adorned (bating the obscene stain of the picric) and so tightly bandaged that he felt his
eyes bulging, she transferred her compassion to the toes. She
scoured the whole phalanx, top and bottom. Suddenly she began to
titter, Belacqua nearly kicked her in the eye, he got such a shock.
How dared she trespass on his programme! He refusing to be
tickled in this petty local way, trying with his teeth to reach his
under-lip and gouging his palms, and she forgetting herself, there
was no other word for it. There were limits, he felt, to Democritus.

'Such a lang tootsy' she giggled.

Heavenly father, the creature was bilingual. A lang tootsy! Belacqua swallowed his choler.

'Soon to be syne' he said in a loud voice. What his repartee lacked
in wit it made up for in style. But it was lost on this granite Medusa.

'A long foot' he said agreeably 'I know, or a long nose. But a long
toe, what does that denote?'

No answer. Was the woman then altogether cretinous? Or did she
not hear him? Belting away there with her urinous picric and cool-
ing her porridge in advance. He would try her again.

'I say' he roared 'that that toe you like so much will soon be only
a memory.' He could not put it plainer than that.

Her voice after his was scarcely audible. It went as follows:

'Yes' — the word died away and was repeated — 'yes, his troubles
are nearly over.'

Belacqua broke down completely, he could not help it. This
distant voice, like a cor anglais coming through the evening, and
then the his, the his was the last straw. He buried his face in his
hands, he did not care who saw him.

'I would like' he sobbed 'the cat to have it, if I might.'

She would never have done with her bandage, it cannot have
measured less than a furlong. But of course it would never do to
leave anything to chance, Belacqua could appreciate that. Still it
seemed somehow disproportioned to the length of even his toe. At
last she made all fast round his shin. Then she packed her tray and
left. Some people go, others leave. Belacqua felt like the rejected of
those two that night in a bed. He felt he had set Miranda somehow

against him. Was this then the haporth of paint? Miranda on whom
so much depended. Merde!

It was all Lister's fault. Those damned happy Victorians.

His heart gave a great leap in its box with a fulminating sense
that he was all wrong, that anger would stand by him better than
the other thing, the laugh seemed so feeble, so like a whinge in the
end. But on second thoughts no, anger would turn aside when it
came to the point, leaving him like a sheep. Anyhow it was too late
to turn back. He tried cautiously what it felt like to have the idea in
his mind. . . . Nothing happened, he felt no shock. So at least he had
spiked the brute, that was something.

At this point he went downstairs and had a truly military evacua-
tion, Army Service Corps. Coming back he did not doubt that all
would yet be well. He whistled a snatch outside the duty-room.
There was nothing left of his room when he got back but Miranda,
Miranda more prognathous than ever, loading a syringe. Belacqua
tried to make light of this.

'What now?' he said.

But she had the weapon into his bottom and discharged before he
realised what was happening. Not a cry escaped him.

'Did you hear what I said?' he said. 'I insist, it is my right, on
knowing the meaning of this, the purpose of this injection, do you
hear me?'

'It is what every patient gets' she said 'before going down to the
theatre.'

Down to the theatre! Was there a conspiracy in this place to
destroy him body and soul? His tongue clave to his palate. They had
desiccated his secretions. First blood to the profession!

The theatre-socks were the next little bit of excitement. Really
the theatre seemed to take itself very seriously. To hell with your
socks, he thought, it's your mind I want.

Now events began to move more rapidly. First of all an angel of
the Lord came to his assistance with a funny story, really very funny
indeed, it always made Belacqua laugh till he cried, about the parson who was invited to take a small part in an amateur production.
All he had to do was to snatch at his heart when the revolver went
off, cry 'By God! I'm shot!' and drop dead. The parson said certainly, he would be most happy, if they would have no objection to

his drawing the line at 'By God' on such a secular occasion. He would replace it, if they had no objection, by 'Mercy!' or 'Upon my word!' or something of that kind. 'Oh my! I'm shot!', how would that be?'

But the production was so amateur that the revolver went off indeed and the man of God was transfixed.

'Oh' he cried 'oh ... ! BY CHRIST! I AM SHOT!'

It was a mercy that Belacqua was a dirty low-down Low Church Protestant high-brow and able to laugh at this sottish jest. Laugh! How he did laugh, to be sure. Till he cried.

He got up and began to titivate himself. Now he could hear the asthmatic breathing if he listened hard. The day was out of danger, any fool could see that. A little sealed cardboard box lying on the mantelpiece caught his eye. He read the inscription: Fraisse's Ferruginous Ampoules for the Intensive Treatment of Anaemia by Intramuscular Squirtation. Registered Trademark — Mozart. The little Hexenmeister of Don Giovanni, now in his narrow cell for ever mislaid, dragged into bloodlessness! How very amusing. Really the world was in great form this morning.

Now two further women, there was no end to them, the one of a certain age, the other not, entered, ripping off their regulation cuffs as they advanced. They pounced on the bed. The precautionary oil-sheet, the cradle ... Belacqua padded up and down before the fire, the ends of his pyjamas tucked like a cyclist's into the sinister socks. He would smoke one more cigarette, nor count the cost. It was astonishing, when he came to think of it, how the entire routine of this place, down to the meanest detail, was calculated to a cow's toe to promote a single end, the relief of suffering in the long run. Observe how he dots his i's now and crucifies his t's to the top of his bent. He was being put to his trumps.

Surreptitiously they searched his yellow face for signs of discomposure. In vain. It was a mask. But perhaps his voice would tremble. One, she whose life had changed, took it upon herself to say in a peevish tone:

'Sister Beamish won't bless you for soiling her good socks.'

Sister Beamish would not bless him.

The voice of this person was in ruins, but she abused it further.

'Would you not stand on the mat?'

His mind was made up in a flash: he would stand on the mat. He would meet them in this matter. If he refused to stand on the mat he was lost in the eyes of these two women.

'Anything' he said 'to oblige Sister Beamish.'

Miranda was having a busy morning. Now she appeared for the fourth or fifth time, he had lost count, complete with shadowy assistants. The room seemed full of grey women. It was like a dream.

'If you have any false teeth' she said 'you may remove them.'

His hour was at hand, there was no blinking at the fact.

Going down in the lift with Miranda he felt his glasses under his hand. This was a blessed accident if you like, just when the silence was becoming awkward.

'Can I trust you with these?' he said.

She put them into her bosom. The divine creature! He would assault her in another minute.

'No smoking' she said 'in the operating-theatre.'

The surgeon was washing his invaluable hands as Belacqua swaggered through the antechamber. He that hath clean hands shall be stronger. Belacqua cut the surgeon. But he flashed a dazzling smile at the Wincarnis. She would not forget that in a hurry.

He bounced up on to the table like a bridegroom. The local doc was in great form, he had just come from standing best man, he was all togged up under his vestments. He recited his exhortation and clapped on the nozzle.

'Are you right?' said Belacqua.

The mixture was too rich, there could be no question about that. His heart was running away, terrible yellow yerks in his skull. 'One of the best,' he heard those words that did not refer to him. The expression reassured him. The best man clawed at his tap.

By Christ! he did die!

They had clean forgotten to auscultate him!

DRAFF

SHUAH, BELACQUA, IN a Nursing Home.

Though this was stale news to Mrs Shuah, for she had inserted it (by telephone) herself, yet she felt, on reading it in the morning after paper, a little shock of surprise, as on opening telegram confirming advance booking in crowded hotel. Then the thought of friends, their unassumed grief giving zest to their bacon and eggs, the first phrases of sympathy with her in this great loss modulating from porridge to marmalade, from whispers and gasps to the calm ejaculations of chat, in a dozen households that she could have mentioned, set in motion through her bodily economy, with results that plainly appeared at once on her face, the wheels of mourning. Whereupon she was without thought or feeling, just a slush, a teary coenaesthesis.

This particular Mrs Shuah, as stated thus far at all events, does not sound very like Thelma née bboggs, nor is she. Thelma née bboggs perished of sunset and honeymoon that time in Connemara. Then shortly after that they suddenly seemed to be all dead, Lucy of course long since, Ruby duly, Winnie to decency, Alba Perdue in the natural course of being seen home. Belacqua looked round and the Smeraldina was the only sail in sight. In next to no time she had made up his mind by not merely loving but wanting him with such quasi-Gorgonesque impatience as her letter precited evinces. She and no other therefore is the Mrs Shuah who now, after less than a year in the ultra-violet intimacy of the compound of ephebe and old woman that he was, reads in the paper that she had begun to survive him.

Bodies don't matter but hers went something like this: big enormous breasts, big breech, Botticelli thighs, knock-knees, square ankles, wobbly, poppata, mammose, slobbery-blubbery, bubbubbub-bub, the real button-busting Weib, ripe. Then, perched away high

out of sight on top of this porpoise prism, the sweetest little pale
Pisanello of a birdface ever. She was like Lucrezia del Fede, pale and
belle, a pale belle Braut, with a winter skin like an old sail in the
wind. The root and the source of the athletic or aesthetic blob of a
birdnose never palled, unless when he had a costive coryza himself,
on Belacqua's forefinger pad and nail, with which he went probing
and plumbing and boring the place just as for many years he pol-
ished his glasses (ecstasy of attrition!), or suffered the shakes and
grace-note strangulations and enthrottlements of the Winkelmusik
of Szopen or Pichon or Chopinek or Chopinetto or whoever it was
embraced her heartily as sure as his name was Fred, dying all his
life (thank you Mr Auber) on a sickroom talent (thank you Mr Field)
and a Kleinmeister's Leiderschaftsucherei (thank you Mr Beckett),
or ascended across the Fulda or the Tolka or the Poddle or the
Volga as the case might be, and he never dreaming that on each and
all of these occasions he was pandering to the most iniquitous ex-
cesses of a certain kind of sublimation. The wretched little wet rag
of an upper lip, pugnozzling up and back in what you might nearly
call a kind of a duck or a cobra sneer to the nostrils, was happily to
some extent amended by the wanton pout of its fellow and the
forward jaws to match — brilliant recovery. The skull of this strapping girl was shaped like a wedge. The ears of course were shells,
the eyes shafts of reseda (his favourite colour) into an oreless mind.
The hair was as black as the pots and grew so thick and low athwart
the temples that the brow was reduced to a fanlight (just the kind
of shaped brow that he most admired). But what matter about
bodies?

She got out of the narrow bed on the wrong side, but she was
never clear in her mind as to which was the right side and which the
wrong, and went into the room where he was laid out, the big bible
wrapped in a napkin still under his chin. She stood at the end of the
bed in her lotus chintz pyjamas, as glazed as those eyes that she
could not see, and held her breath. His forehead, when she ventured
to lay the back of her hand across it, was much less chilly than she
had expected, but that no doubt was explained by her own periph-
eral circulation, which was wretched. She caught hold of his hands,
folded, not on his breast as she would have wished, but lower down,
and rearranged them. Scarcely had she gone down on her bended

knees after having made this adjustment when a spasm of anxiety,
lest there should be anything the matter with this corpse that rigor
mortis had apparently passed over, straightened her up. She hoped
it was all right. Baulked of her prayer, baulked of a last long look at
the disaffected face, its contemptuous probity that would fall to
pieces, she took herself off to prepare her weeds, for it would not
do to be seen in lotus chintz. Black suited her, black and green had
always been her colours. She found in her room what she had in
mind, an Ethiope one-piece gashed and slashed with emerald insert-
ions. She brought it to her work-table in the penannular bow-win-
dow, she sat down trembling and began to fix it. It was like being up
in the sky in a bubble, the sun streaming in (through the curtains),
the blue all round her. Soon the floor was strewn with the bright
cuttings, it went to her heart to rip them they looked so lovely. Not
a flower, not a flower sweet.

> One insertion in the Press
> Makes minus how many to make a black dress?

She was so sad and busy, the sobs were so quick to ripen and
burst in her mind and the work was so nice, that she did not notice
a fat drab demon approach the house nor hear his uproarious endeavours not to intrude on the gravel. Up came his card. Mr Malacoda. Most respectfully desirous to measure. A sob, instead of bursting, withered. The Smeraldina whimpered that she was sorry but
she could not admit this Mr Malacoda, she could not have the
Master measured. Mary Ann's leprous features were much abused
with the usual. In a crisis like this, however, she was worth ten or
fifteen of her mistress.

'He'd be about the Master's size' she said.

Just fancy her noticing that!

'Then why don't you tell him so' moaned the Smeraldina 'and let
do the best he can and not be coming up here to torment me.'

What could an inch or so possibly matter this way or that? There
was no question of having to skimp aragonite or peperino. The
coffin was not going to eat him.

Mary Ann returned to the torment with the sad news that Mr
Malacoda was at that very moment springing up the stairs with a

tape in his black claws. The Smeraldina started up, clutching the scissor, and began to plunge towards the door. But the thought of the thoral chintz brought her up short. Had again!

'You might at least bring me a cup of tea' she said.

Mary Ann left the room.

'And a lightly boiled egg' cried the Smeraldina.

A small wreath, of arum lilies needless to say, arrived in a box – anonymous. This the Smeraldina buried. She sought out the gardener, a slow shy slob of a man with a dripping moustache, and found him watering in a dazed and hopeless manner a bed of blighted sweet-william. Someone had stolen his rose, he mowed down the flowers with hard jets of water. She sent him flying up into the heart of the mountains with two sacks to gather bracken. Then he might go home. Herself she stripped a eucalyptus of its boughs.

The parson came churning up the avenue in bottom gear, confirmed his worst fears with a quick look at the windows, let fall his rustless all-steel in sorrow and anger on the gravel, and walked right in.

'I never knew anyone founder' he declared in a passionate way, 'and I've seen a good many.'

'No' said the Smeraldina.

'Automatic dispensation' he cried. 'Strength from on high' snapping his thumb 'like that. Meet in Paradize.'

'Yes' said the Smeraldina.

'No sooner does he arrive' clasping his hands and looking up (why up?) 'there where there is no time, than you burst in upon him.'

'He's all right' said the Smeraldina. 'I know that.'

'Therefore be glad' cried the parson.

He pedalled away like a weaver's shuttle (but not before she had covenanted to be glad) to administer the Eucharist, of which he always carried an abundance in a satchel on the bracket of his bike, to a moneyed wether up the road whose tale was nearly told. Seven and six a time.

Capper Quin arrived on tiptire, in a car of his very own. He grappled with the widow, he simply could not help it. She was a sensible girl in some ways, she was not ashamed to let herself go in the arms of a man of her own weight at last. They broke away,

carrot plucked from tin of grease, and Hairy stood humbly before
her, hers to command. He was greatly improved, commerce with the
things of time had greatly improved him. Now he could speak quite
nicely, he did not simply have to abandon his periods in despair
after a word or two.

She stood by while he freighted the car. The sacks distended with
fern and bracken; the boughs of eucalyptus, piecemeal to meet the
occasion, tied up in an old stable jacket; a superb shrub of verbena
treated in the same way; a vat of moss; a bag of wire tholes. When
all these things had been safely stowed and the car pointed in the
right direction, Hairy followed her lead into the house and took up
position, the crutch well split, the great feet splayed, swollen paws
appaumée two dangling chunks of blood ballast, aborted mammae
much in evidence, at gaze. Even Ireland has a few animals, now
generally regarded as varieties, which have been ranked as species
by some zoologists. He felt his face improving as grief modelled the
features.

'Might I see him?' he whispered, like a priest asking for a book in
the Trinity College Library.

She had herself supported up the stairs, she led the way into the
death-chamber as though it belonged to her. They diverged, the body
was between them on the bed like the keys between nations in
Velasquez's Lances, like the water between Buda and Pest, and so
on, hyphen of reality.

'Very beautiful' said Hairy.

'I think very' said the Smeraldina.

'They all are' said Hairy.

Shed a tear, damn you, she thought, I can't. But he went one better, he choked a whole bucketful back. His face improved rapidly.

They met again at the foot of the bed, like parallels made to for
the sake of argument, and occupied this fresh viewpoint with heads
together until the Smeraldina, feeling the absurdity of the position,
detached herself, left the room and closed the door behind her, on
the dying and the dead.

Hairy felt it was up to him now to feel something.

'You are quieter than humus' he said in his mind, 'you will give
the bowels of the earth a queer old lesson in quiet.'

That was the best he could manage at the time. But bowels surely was hardly the right word. That was where Queen Anne had the gout.

The hands pious on the sternum were unseemly, defunct crusader, absolved from polite campaign. Hairy reached out with his endless arms and tugged at the marble members. Two nouns and two adjectives. Not a stir out of them. How stupid of him.

'This is final' he thought.

Belacqua had often looked forward to meeting the girls, Lucy especially, hallowed and transfigured beyond the veil. What a hope! Death had already cured him of that naïvete.

Hairy, anxious though he was to rejoin the Smeraldina while his face was at its best, before it relapsed into the workaday dumpling, steak and kidney pudding, had his work cut out to tear himself away. For he could not throw off the impression that he was letting slip a rare occasion to feel something really stupendous, something that nobody had ever felt before. But time pressed. The Smeraldina was pawing the ground, his own personal features were waning (or perhaps better, waxing). In the end he took his leave without kneeling, without a prayer, but his brain quite prostrate and suppliant before this first fact of its experience. That was at least something. He would have welcomed a long Largo, on the black notes for preference.

In the cemetery the light was failing, the sea moonstone washing the countless toes turned up, the mountains swarthy Uccello behind the headstones. The loveliest little lap of earth you ever saw. Hairy shifted the roof of planks from off the brand-new pit and went down, down, down the narrow steps carefully not removed by the groundsmen. His head came to rest below the surface of the earth. What a nerve the man had to be sure. The significance of this was lost on the Smeraldina, she merely crouched on the brink.

Well, to make a long story short, the pair of them between them, she feeding him from above, upholstered the grave: the floor with moss and fern, the walls with the verdure outstanding. Low down the clay was so hard that Hairy had to take his shoe to the tholes. However they made a great job of it, not a spot of clay showed when they had gone, all was lush, green and most sweet smelling.

But soon it would be black and dark night, a chill wind arose, the pangs of light began on the foothills, and moonstone turned to ashes. The Smeraldina shivered, as well she might. Hairy, taking a last look round at his handiwork, was as snug as a bug in a rug. Belacqua lay dead on the bed with the timeless mock on the face. Hairy came up out of the hole, drew up the steps behind him, put back the planks and rubbed his hands with a sigh, labour ended, labour of love, painful duty.

All of a sudden the groundsman was there, a fine man in ruins, as drunk as he knew how, giving point to the consecrated ground. He was most moved by their attentions, without parallel in his experience of the forsaken. For his own part he could be relied on to work himself to the bone for the defunct, whom he had known well, not only as a man, but as a boy, also. The Smeraldina had a quick vision of Belacqua as a boy, shinning up the larch trees, his breast expanding to the world.

Hairy feeling father, brother, husband, confessor, friend of the family (what family?) and the inevitable something more, did the heavy with the reeling groundsman. The Smeraldina played up. Belacqua, idealised something horrid, made the widow and her huge escort, who now stalked off, four lovely deaf ears, faces tilted slightly to the starry sky, one in this sordid matter.

'Home Hairy' she said.

Hairy quickened his step, enveloped her, helped her along.

'I don't see the moon' she said.

Like a jack-in-the-box the satellite obliged, let down her shining ladder to the shore. She had a long lonely climb before her.

The groundsman, cut to the quick, mindful of his lumbago, sat down on the planks and lowered his bottle of stout. Guinness for Thinness, stultifying stout. He had lost interest in all the shabby mysteries, he was beyond caring. He strained his ear for the future, his future, and what did he hear? All the ancient punctured themes recurring, creeping up the treble out of sound. Very well. Let the essence of his being stay where it was, in liquor and liquor's harmonics, accepted gladly as the ultimate expression of his nonchalance. He rose and made his water agin a cypress.

That night Hairy lay in his bed, tossed and turned for various reasons, fell off at last into a troubled sleep, woke not at all refreshed to a day of wind and rain, the weather having broken in the small hours.

At midday to the Smeraldina, in bed indulging her most secret thoughts, salivating slightly for a lightly boiled egg, Mary Ann appeared. Mr Malacoda. Keen to coffin. The Smeraldina observed in a bitter voice that if the man must coffin why coffin he must, surely there was no clear call on Mary Ann to make a point of pestering her with what could not be cured.

A thin wall, a good but thin wall, separated her from Mr Malacoda and assistant ungulata, in a fever to have done. Cerements did not suit the defunct, with their riot of frills and lace they made him look like a pantomime baby.

When Hairy arrived it was the magic hour, Homer dusk, when the subliminal rats come abroad on their rounds. The little something extra that he felt he had come in for made great strides at the expense of its co-heirs. He agreed absolutely that cerements did not suit the defunct, somehow they made him look so put-upon and helpless, almost as though he had not done dying. He stayed to supper.

A point to bear in mind is that the Smeraldina was so naturally happy-go-lucky that she did not find it at all easy to feel deeply, or rather, perhaps better, be deeply sentimental. Her life had been springing leaks for as long as she cared to remember. A husband — and how! — was oakum in the end the same as everything else, prophylactic, a wire bandage of Jalade-Lafont. Belacqua had come unstuck like his own favour of veronica in What a Misfortune. Losers seekers. The position was not quite so simple as all that, there was some sentimental factor in play (or at work) complicating the position, but that was more or less it.

That night the weather so mended as to be more than merely clement for the ceremony. Malacoda and Co. turned up bright and early with their six cylinder hearse, black as Ulysses's cruiser. The demon, quite unable to control his impatience to cover, could only manage a quick flirt with Mary Ann. The Smeraldina was through with the death-chamber, not that she was callous, quite the reverse, but the livery of death, leaving aside its pale flag altogether, was too much for her. Hairy, more and more self-assured servitor, was of the same opinion. So let the good man cover by all means. That was what he was there for, that was what he was paid for. Let the whole nightmare brood walk up by all manner of means.

Now he was grinning up at the lid at last.

'No flowers' said Hairy.

God forbid!

'And no friends.'

Need he ask!

The parson arrived in the nick of time. He had been casting out devils all morning, he was in a muck sweat.

Hairy scampered out into the sunlight and the balmy breeze, free of the house that was suddenly jerry-built mausoleum, with a message from his sweet ward to the driver whose name was Scarmiglione, a strongly worded message exhorting him to temper full speed with due caution. 'Let her out' said Hairy in his pretentious jargon 'to the irreducible coefficient of safety.' Scarmiglione met this request with a look of petrified courtesy. On these trips he deferred to the speed-controlling washer of his own mind and conscience, and to none other. He was adamant in this matter. Hairy shrank away from the affable rictus.

All aboard. All sounds at half-mast. Aye-aye.

Mary Ann found the gardener shut up in the tool-shed, all of a heap on an upturned box, nervously tying knots in a piece of raffia. He was not neglecting his work, he was grieving.

'The only one' said Mary Ann, alluding to their late employer, 'as ever I dreamed on', as though that could possibly interest the gardener. But what higher tribute could she pay? The gardener had secured his retreat, she could not come at him, she could only hold her livid farthing of a face at the broken window and commit copious nuisance with her opinions and impressions. She did not expect an answer, she did not pause for one, she received none. He heard the voice at a great distance, but could make no sense of it. For he was, temporarily at all events, just a clod of gloom, in which concern for his own state of health counted for more than he would have cared to admit. Was he overdoing things about the place? It was hard to say. He heard Mary Ann in the run, her voice raised in furious hallali, butchering a fowl for the table. He began to look about for his line. Some unauthorised person had taken his line, with the result that now he was helpless to put down his broccoli. He rose and let himself out, he slobbered out of darkness into light, he chose a place in the sun and settled, he was like a colossal fly trimming its load of typhus. Gradually he cheered up. Ten to one God was in his heaven.

Though the grave was deep the committal was neat, not a hitch; its words perhaps a trifle misdirected on the vile, the sure and certain hope rather gobbled up in the fact of departure. The tone conveyed to 'earth to earth' was a triumph of passionate and contemptuous reproach to all the living. How dared they continue full of misery! Pah!

'Now in Gaelic' said Hairy on the way home 'they could not say that.'

'What could they not say?' said the parson. He would not rest until he knew.

'O Death where is thy sting?' replied Hairy. 'They have no words for these big ideas.'

This was more than enough for the parson, a canon of the Church of Ireland, who hastily exclaimed, no doubt by way of a shining straw, to the Smeraldina:

'My wife would so much like to see you.'

'O Anthrax' said Hairy 'where is thy pustule?'

'She has been through the fire' said the parson, 'she understands. My poor dear mother-in-law!'

'O G.P.I.' said Hairy 'where are thy rats?'

By the mercy of God the good canon was slow to wrath.

'And so on' said Hairy 'and so forth. They can't say it once and for all. A spalpeen's babble.'

Belacqua dead and buried, Hairy seemed to have taken on a new lease of life. He spoke well, with commendable assurance; he looked better, less obese cretin and spado than ever before; and he felt better, which was a great thing. Perhaps the explanation of this was that while Belacqua was alive Hairy could not be himself, or, if you prefer, could be nothing else. Whereas now the defunct, such of his parts at least as might be made to fit, could be pressed into service, incorporated in the daily ellipses of Capper Quin without his having to face the risk of exposure. Already Belacqua was not wholly dead, but merely mutilated. The Smeraldina appreciated this without thinking.

As for her, it was almost as though she had suffered the inverse change. She had died in part. She had definitely ceased to exist in that particular part which Belacqua had been at such pains to isolate, the public part so cruelly made private for his convenience, her least clandestine aspect[1] reduced to a radiograph and exploited to ginger his secret occasions. That was down the mine Daddy with the dead Sadomasochist. Her spiritual equivalent, to give it a name, had been measured, coffined and covered by Nick Malacoda. As material for anagogy (Greek g if you don't mind) the worms were welcome to her.

What was left was just a fine strapping lump of a girl or woman, theatre nurse in Yellow from the neck down, bursting with Lebensgeist at every suture, itching to be taken at her – very much so to speak – face value, and by force for preference.

Now it so happened that these two processes, a kind of marginal metabolism possibly you might call them, independent but of common origin, constructive in the case of the man, destructive and delightfully excrementitious in the case of the woman, culminated and simultaneously on the drive back from the grave.

Hairy stopped the car.

'Step down' he said to the parson, 'I don't like you.'

The parson appealed mutely to the Smeraldina. She had nothing whatever to say to him. Never again in this life would she occupy any position more partisan than that of a comfortably covered bone of contention, her mind was made up.

'Bill the executors' said Hairy 'and out you hop.'

The parson did as Hairy bid. He felt miserable. They did not even give him a chance to cock up the other cheek. He racked his brains for coals of fire. As the car began to move away he jumped up nimbly on the running-board, stooped forward in the lee of the windscreen and began, heedless of punctuation, in a lamentable voice:

'. . . no more death neither sorrow nor crying neither shall there be any more—'

At which point, the car beginning to sway in a perilous manner, he was obliged to break off in order to save his life. He stood in the road, far from home, and hoped, without exactly making a prayer out of it, that they might be forgiven.

[1] What a competent poet once called the bella menzogna.

'Wouldn't he give you the sick' said Hairy 'with his Noo Gefoozleum.'

Little remains to be told. On their return they found the house in flames, the home to which Belacqua had brought three brides a raging furnace. It transpired that during their absence something had snapped in the brain of the gardener, who had ravished the servant girl and then set the premises on fire. He had neither given himself up nor tried to escape, he had shut himself up in the toolshed and awaited arrest.

'Ravished Mary Ann' exclaimed the Smeraldina.

'So she deposes' said a high official of the Civic Guard. 'It was she who raised the alarm.'

Hairy looked this dignitary up and down.

'I don't see your fiddle' he said.

'Where is the girl?' asked the Smeraldina.

'She has gone home to her Mother' answered the high official.

She tried him again.

'Where is the gardener?'

But he had been expecting this question.

'He resisted arrest, he has been taken to hospital.'

'Where are the heroes of the fire-brigade' said Hairy, entering into the spirit of the thing, 'the boys of the old brigade, the Tara Street Cossacks? May we expect them to-day? They would act as a kind of antiphlogistic.'

This Hairy was a revelation to the Smeraldina, he was indeed hairy.

'They are unavoidably detained' replied the Commissioner.

'Take me away' said the Smeraldina firmly, 'the house is insured.'

The Commissioner made a mental note of this suspicious circumstance.

Poor Smeraldina! She was more than ever at a loose end now.

'Why not come with me' said Hairy, 'now that all this has happened, and be my love?'

'I don't understand' said the Smeraldina.

Hairy explained exactly what he meant. In the heart of the purple mountains the car conked out. Hairy had exhausted his petrol supply. But nothing daunted he continued to explain. He explained and explained, the same old thing over and over again. At last he too conked out.

'Perhaps after all' murmured the Smeraldina 'this is what darling Bel would wish.'

'What is?' cried Hairy aghast.

She handed him back his explanation in a nutshell.

'Darling Smerry!' cried Hairy. 'What else?'

They fell silent. Hairy, gazing straight before him through the anti-dazzle windscreen, whose effect by the way on the mountains was to make them look not unlike the picture by Paul Henry, was inclined to think that it was about time they started to make a move. But this seemed out of the question. The Smeraldina, far far away with the corpse and her own spiritual equivalent in the boneyard by the sea, was dwelling at length on how she would shortly gratify the former, even as it, while still unfinished, had that of Lucy,[1] and blot the latter for ever from his memory.

'We must think of an inscription' she said.

'He did mention one to me once' said Hairy, 'now that I come to think of it, that he would have endorsed, but I can't recall it.'

The groundsman stood deep in thought. What with the company of headstones sighing and gleaming like bones, the moon on the job, the sea tossing in her dreams and panting, and the hills observing their Attic vigil in the background, he was at a loss to determine off-hand whether the scene was of the kind that is termed romantic or whether it should not with more justice be deemed classical. Both elements were present, that was indisputable. Perhaps classico-romantic would be the fairest estimate. A classico-romantic scene.

Personally he felt calm and wistful. A classico-romantic working-man therefore. The words of the rose to the rose floated up in his mind: 'No gardener has died, comma, within rosaceous memory.' He sang a little song, he drank his bottle of stout, he dashed away a tear, he made himself comfortable.

So it goes in the world.

[1] A most foully false analogy.

Samuel Beckett
Murphy 50p

A brilliant tragi-comic novel of an Irishman's adventures in London. By the Nobel Prizewinner who is 'one of the greatest prose-writers of the century' TIMES LITERARY SUPPLEMENT

Flann O'Brien
The Best of Myles £1·00

'Myles na Gopaleen' was the name Flann O'Brien adopted for Cruiskeen Lawn, the column he wrote for the *Irish Times*. This book is a selection of the best of that material — and it is one of the supreme comic achievements in our language — containing such immortal creations as The Brother, a man with a solution to everything from the common cold to the economic crisis; and Keats and Chapman, two absurdly erudite poets who will stoop to any old adventure so long as it ends in an epigram.

The Dalkey Archive 75p

Dalkey, a little town maybe twelve miles south of Dublin, is the setting for such characters as Augustine, James Joyce and a man who is in danger of turning into a bicycle. The deeply religious Mrs Laverty presides over the Colza Hotel. De Selby, the mad scientist, who achieves further fame in *The Third Policeman*, discovers how to make magnificent whiskey in a week. Mick and Hackett compete for the favours of Mary. This is surely one of Flann O'Brien's finest comedies.

The Hard Life 75p

Into the household of Mr Collopy come two orphan boys. While Mr Collopy is engaged in mysterious humanitarian work on behalf of women, the boys grow up in the odour of good whiskey and bad cooking. Manus progresses from teaching people by post how to walk the tightrope to running his 'London University Academy'. His younger brother, Finbarr, watches and waits . . .

The Third Policeman 75p

This novel is comparable only to *Alice in Wonderland* as an allegory of the absurd. It is a murder thriller, a hilarious comic satire about an archetypal village police force, a surrealistic vision of eternity, and a tender, brief, erotic story about the unrequited love affair between a man and his bicycle.

Russell Hoban

'He is an original, imaginative and inventive. Though some of his work has been compared with that of Tolkien and C. S. Lewis, he is his own man, working his own vein of magical fantasy' MAURICE WIGGIN, SUNDAY TIMES

Turtle Diary 80p

In the aquarium at the London Zoo, three sea turtles swim endlessly in 'their little bedsitter of ocean'. Two lonely people, William G. and Neaera H., become obsessed with the turtles' captivity, and resolve to rescue them and release them in the sea.

William's and Neaera's diaries tell the story of how they achieve the turtles' freedom, and in the process re-define their own lives . . .

The Lion of Boaz-Jachin and Jachin-Boaz 60p

Russell Hoban writes of a time in which there are no lions any more. Middle-aged Jachin-Boaz, the map-seller, leaves his wife, taking with him the map that was to give his son, Boaz-Jachin a start in life. The boy performs rites at the palace of a long-dead king, and far away the father wakes one morning to find a lion waiting for him in the street.

Painful, funny, vivid with the desperate detail of life, this is a book which goes beyond the ordinary range of experience into a new realm of the imagination.

Kleinzeit 80p

On a day like any other, Kleinzeit gets fired, is booked into hospital for a recurring pain, falls in love with a beautiful night sister, and finds himself pitched headlong into a wild and flickering world of mystery . . .

Richard Brautigan
The Hawkline Monster 75p

In the dead centre of the Dead Hills of Eastern Oregon stands Hawkline
Manor, an elaborate Victorian mansion, festooned with chandeliers and
valuable paintings, and looked after by a giant butler. It is the home of the
two Miss Hawklines, beautiful, generous with their favours — and identical.
But it also houses a very unwelcome guest . . . whom Greer and Cameron,
professional killers, are required to dispose of.

Trout Fishing in America 75p

A miraculous journey through a country and a mind, by a dazzling young
American writer. 'A minor classic' THE TIMES

In Watermelon Sugar 75p

Luminous, spellbinding story of the people who live near iDEATH, where
the sun shines a different colour every day. The marvellous successor to
Trout Fishing in America

Revenge of the Lawn 75p

Sixty-two fantasies, love stories and reminiscences of San Francisco and
Tacoma . . . 'like prose poems or modern folk tales' GUARDIAN

You can buy these and other Pan books from booksellers and
newsagents; or direct from the following address:
Pan Books, Cavaye Place, London SW10 9PG
Send purchase price plus 15p for the first book and 5p for
each additional book, to allow for postage and packing
Prices quoted are applicable in UK

While every effort is made to keep prices low, it is sometimes
necessary to increase prices at short notice. Pan Books reserve the
right to show on covers new retail prices which may differ
from those advertised in the text or elsewhere